Rise

Diamondsong

A Concerto in Ten Parts

Part 10:
Rise

E.D.E. Bell

Atthis Arts
Detroit, Michigan

Diamondsong
Part 10: Rise

This is a work of fiction.
Any resemblance to actual pyrsi, winged or otherwise, is purely coincidental.

Cover Art by M.C. Krauss

Map of Ada-ji by Ulla Thynell

Interior Design by G.C. Bell

Editorial Services by:
Catherine Jones Payne, Quill Pen Editorial
Kelsey Ronan
M. Cusack

Published by Atthis Arts, LLC
Detroit, Michigan
atthisarts.com

ISBN 978-1-945009-66-2

Library of Congress Control Number: 2020945199

First Edition: Published October 2020

This book is dedicated to G.C. Bell.

I love that you're you.

PREFACE

Thank you so much for being here with me. Given how much I had to navigate to get this serial completed, I just hope that, in its spirit and its flaws, it has meant something to its readers.

We left off on the last preface with me in slight catharsis trying to get too many things out in a short space. I kept editing it, but the text was already busting out of the margins. I'll note that there were a few points I wish I could have addressed with a bit more nuance, but in the interest of letting what's done be so, I will hope that several implicit caveats were apparent and move along. Because, look, we have reached the end!

Given all else, my approach to this last volume was to write it as authentically as I could, and not worry about other ways it could be, or what people might expect of it. But I do want to get a few things on the record. While it revels in gender freedom, *Diamondsong* is not about gender—at least not in *their* world—and it is not about race. Race is appropriately inseparable from our current conversations, but it is not an intended metaphor in Ada-ji, which has species but not races. It is also not about one side of the cliff at large oppressing the another. It isn't left and right or two sides.

It's supposed to be more subtle than that. And I don't want to spell out all the layers and themes. I want readers to discover and consider them, as they will speak differently to different people.

I will also note that the serial was drafted and almost entirely edited before this year's pandemic. (Finishing during that time was a *thing*, in addition to what I am about to tell you.) So the story was not meant to address that, though some elements resonate (and some resonate differently) in its midst. In fact, the Part 08 preface had been written with a fully positive tone (Finally! I'd felt proud of this!), and I had to change it last minute, as we went to press with the world swirling in uncertainty and lockdown.

I was also unaware, as we went to print Part 08, that I personally was a few days away from my own mental collapse. A culmination of chronic, repeating issues, but one too many push and one too many fall, this time. Apropos to the following release of *Depths*, certainly, but there was nothing fictional about it. I don't think this is the right place to tell the story, and it's rather complicated anyway. But my life is changed, and I'm only starting to move forward and understand the facets of that.

It's always been something these last years, in so many spheres, from the smallest to the largest. Perhaps, when the literary history of 2017-2020 is examined, *Diamondsong* could be included in that discussion. I would like that.

Diamondsong was never written to be an answer, nor do I consider it one. It is a conversation. Maybe you won't agree with one of the characters. You'll think xe went too far or not far enough or xe should have changed course. Or you'll think my phrasing implied something problematic. Humanity is complicated, and part of improving it, as a whole and for each of us, is exploring it. As I now understand, I wrote this serial through growing impacts of multiple (and at the time, untreated) severe mental health issues, through my own lenses and trauma—and I did my best. There is growth in the art, and searching, and I think that is relevant. It's ok to see it. Talk about it. In fact, I worry knowing that some of the more thoughtful minds I've encountered are not writing, or not speaking, because they feel they are expected to do so perfectly, to everyone's expectations. It's an issue.

What do I hope you've taken from this serial? I hope you've enjoyed the journey. I wanted it to feel like a storytime, which doesn't need to be so sculpted, and not every hair gets braided.

Sometimes wandering, but with a desire to know where the road might lead. And, as I've said, I wanted it to feel like a conversation—this might seem odd since only I wrote it, but I do feel that way. Of course, there was an entire community of editors and early readers. But also, you interact with me online. In person. You may think on your own about what you've read and how it applies to your life or the world around us, and that is an important part of that dialogue.

As for me, I've changed so much. Eight years ago, I set out clueless and confident, because I needed an escape. Desperately. And the world that I found helped knock those remaining layers away, one by one, but it did not resolve the healing that I needed. And that is where I start now. Now, having set out to complete the works I originally planned, and having actually left my previous career, and with a whole indie press on the brink, and with a more realistic vision of myself and our world, and with an entirely redefined set of personal challenges to face, I'm not a different person but sometimes I feel like one. Open-eyed. Bruised. Disillusioned. Kind of—*scared*. Also—*hopeful*. So now what?

Writing this way about these subjects with who I am and with this past and with this mind is hard, and it's vulnerable, but I love this world, and I want to be a part of it, and I want to be a part of it as me, connecting here with you. I am going to do my best to write—and write in my authentic voice—for as long as I am able and feel I have something to contribute. I will be Emily. I will talk about compassion. I will encourage kindness. I will welcome people to this discussion. I will encourage people both to listen and to think for themselves. To be connected. I will encourage people to question what they've learned. To see each other's journeys. To understand nuance. To care for themselves. Something like that, right? And I will do it with as much love and light as I can muster. When we're not sure about something, we can discuss it, and learn from each other. I can't live—or write—in fear of unkindness. I can only do my best to be kind, to myself also, and to continue to grow and learn in appropriate measure. I will know my friends are standing with me. And I with them.

I appreciate you. You give me strength. You give me will. We'll lift each other from the depths and together we will rise.

Again, I must thank the team that saw this final volume through. My gratitude to Catherine Jones Payne and Kelsey Ronan. To Meghan Cusack, Camille Gooderham Campbell, Sasha Kasoff Moore, Laura Johnson, Deborah Reilly, and Maria Judge. To my departed friends, Trowby Brockman and Al McKenzie—who continue to influence me every day. And to the people who have helped me through this year: all of you, but in particular also Leda Scurrell, Valerie Linebaugh, Nancy Bell (Mom B), Lois Reynolds, Marsalis, and of course Chris, Gwynn, Vance, Vera, and Mura.

This concludes the gem trilogy. My tutorial is done. It's been exactly seven years, five novels, eleven novellas, three anthologies, and an assortment of short stories since that first release. And I'm eager now to try something new, universe willing. Totally with dragons. ☺

I hope you enjoy the ending. And I hope it will bring a happy beginning.

I care about you all so much. Thanks for reading my story. Perhaps you will consider it our story.

Love to you and best wishes to our future,

E.D.E. Bell

October 2020

THE WORLD OF ADA-JI

The Ja-lal: A humanoid species, dwelling in the foothills and plains of Ada-ji, characterized by broad advancements in construction, invention, and health. The Fo-ror call them brutes.

The Fo-ror: A winged humanoid species, dwelling in the forests of Ada-ji, characterized by their natural living and the use of magical powers, known as valence. The Ja-lal call them fairies.

The Ja-lal and Fo-ror are similar in form, with gray skin, but differences between them in composition and culture. Pyr is singular for a Ja-lal or Fo-ror and pyrsi is plural.

The pyrsi of Ada-ji hold many **gender identities**. While this doesn't clarify all aspects of gender, it is polite to introduce oneself with a prefix, indicating the appropriate pronouns:

Fe' indicates a set of feminine identities, using the pronouns she/her/her(s).

Ma' indicates a set of masculine identities, using the pronouns he/him/his.

Ji' indicates a set of spectrum identities, using the pronouns ve/ver/vis.

When gender is unknown, it is polite to refer to a pyr with xe/xem/xyr(s). Any group of pyrsi (plural) would be referred to with they/them/their(s).

A pyr may be generically referred to as **Burge**, short for the more formal Burgess, often for purposes of polite address or getting a stranger's attention. This is similar to the use of Sir or Ma'am on Earth. For those who hold social prejudice based on class, the term implies some sense of status or honor.

Ja-lal and Fo-ror may live up to 50 cycles. Their lives are divided into defined **epochs**, aligning with societal expectations:

Aoch — Age 0-9 — Characterized by upbringing, education, and exploration

Bakh — Age 10-19 — Centered on building family, performing and completing apprenticeships, and finalizing life plans

Gamh — Age 20-29 — Fully immersed in their specialty or role, contributing full-time to society

Dorh — Age 30-39 — Respected in leadership and/or advisory roles; it is normal to take some time for self

Eroh — Age 40+ — Expected to retire and engage in craft or occasional consulting, through the **life expectancy of around 50 cycles**.

Expectations differ for each culture. For example, while a Ja-lal must develop xyr profession into a career, a Fo-ror's profession and rank are set based on xyr social class and other historical and cultural factors.

A **cycle** on Ada-ji is perhaps up to four times the length of an Earth year. So, our main character, at age 20.5 cycles, has lived more than 80 Earth years but, in relation to her life span, could be considered at the **maturity of her early forties** on Earth.

Each **turn** on Ada-ji, a period of day and then night, is **significantly longer than an Earth day**. As such, pyrsi do not sleep according to light or dark, but instead based on their own needs, lifestyle, profession, and schedule.

The Ja-lal measure time by the periodic sounding of bells; they refer to the resultant time periods with the same term. The Fo-ror are less rigid about time-keeping and refer to the equivalent time period as a span. Each **bell**, or **span**, consists of more than two Earth hours.

Smaller amounts of time are referred to by both cultures as **takes**, which can be thought of as about ten Earth minutes.

In Earth terms, it has been about eight weeks since the beginning of our tale.

The Ja-lal and Fo-ror live on separate sides of the Great Cliff. They have not interacted since the ***Great War***, an event most noted for being the **end of the Violence** on Ada-ji.

Synopsis to Here

Just after Dime had left her career working for the Circles, the government of the Ja-lal, three hooded figures burst into her home, determined to take her away. Dime and her spouse, Dayn, ran to escape them.

The intruders were revealed to be Fo-ror, commonly called fairies. These fairies, unseen since the conclusion of the Great War, were feared and loathed by the Ja-lal, who were taught that any contact would cause the Violence to return.

Dime escaped the city and was rescued by a large animal species known as newts, where she befriended a young newt she called Juni. Dime was found there by a fe'pyr familiar with fairies, Ella, who broke the news that Dime was biologically a Fo-ror—one whose wings had been removed.

Later, Ella explained that the magical fairy power of valence did not come from the wings, but from the heart. At her recommendation, Dime traveled to the diamond caves, where she confirmed and practiced her powers. There, she discovered that the Ja-lal also have powers of valence, more internally directed. Dime believes very few Ja-lal are aware of, and thus intentionally shaping, their own powers.

Trying to make sense of these events, Dime traveled between the lands of the fairies, the Heartland, and her own Sol's Reach. She reconnected with friends: Zael, who is dying, Ador, the founder of an advocacy group called the Free Winds, Ador's spouse Batu, and Dime's own family: Dayn, Luja, and Tum. She was surprised to run into Rock, an Intel Agent and former flame, with whom she has developed a complicated friendship.

She encountered new allies: Volana, a fairy connected to a secret Fo-ror discussion group, the Foundry, Volana's friend Uchitar, who struggles with tzetz-addiction, and Hin, a young assistant Ador had taken under his charge, whose reservations about working with the fairies culminated in an incident of rudeness toward Dime.

While in the Heartland, Dime was approached by an officer of a political group, the Risers, named Intinpalo. He believes in the superiority of the Fo-ror, but an encounter with Dime's father, Gorg, may have left an impression.

Dime has met with the leaders of each land. First, High Seat Ferala, who confessed that Dime was part of an old scheme to avenge the horrors of a disease called the curse, which the Fo-ror blamed on the Ja-lal. This scheme, designed by now Third Seat Neimano, was named Project Diamondsong. His plan was to remove the wings from Fo-ror newborns, place them in positions of potential influence amongst the Ja-lal, and then allow them to grow up before activating their loyalties as Fo-ror spies. Twice, she has met with Sala, the Light, who remains resistant to her message of working with the Fo-ror.

Dime has been able to locate four other victims of Neimano: Kolk, Nafat, Olok, and Jaza, the leader of the Sol's Pillars herself.

Additionally, Dime has learned that the newts hold emotion-based valence. Stern Eyes used hers to shock Neimano, causing him to fly away, clearly injured, after he tried to attack Dime once again.

After thinking about comments Jaza had made, Dime decided she needed to find out more about Neimano's plans. She and Rock returned to the Heartland, where Tikinal, the Seats' High Clerk, directed them to meet with a secretive agent. This agent told them that Neimano was hiding a weapon: perhaps vials containing the deadly curse.

Together: Dime, Rock, Uchitar, Luja, Stern Eyes, and Juni found Neimano's secret room. Low on stamina, Uchitar had taken some more of the drug tzetz, and Luja gave him more to keep him from crashing. Luja realized it was not the curse that the room held, but a serum, intended to rekindle the dormant virus within the victims. Luja insisted on keeping Dime away, and ve destroyed it instead. But Dime now understands Neimano's plan—she was the intended weapon. One way or another.

With the boring continuing above, the group barely made it past Neimano's attacks and back to the borrowed space in Pito, where Volana, Tum, Ador, and the kita Agni were waiting. Ador has just stated that he has news.

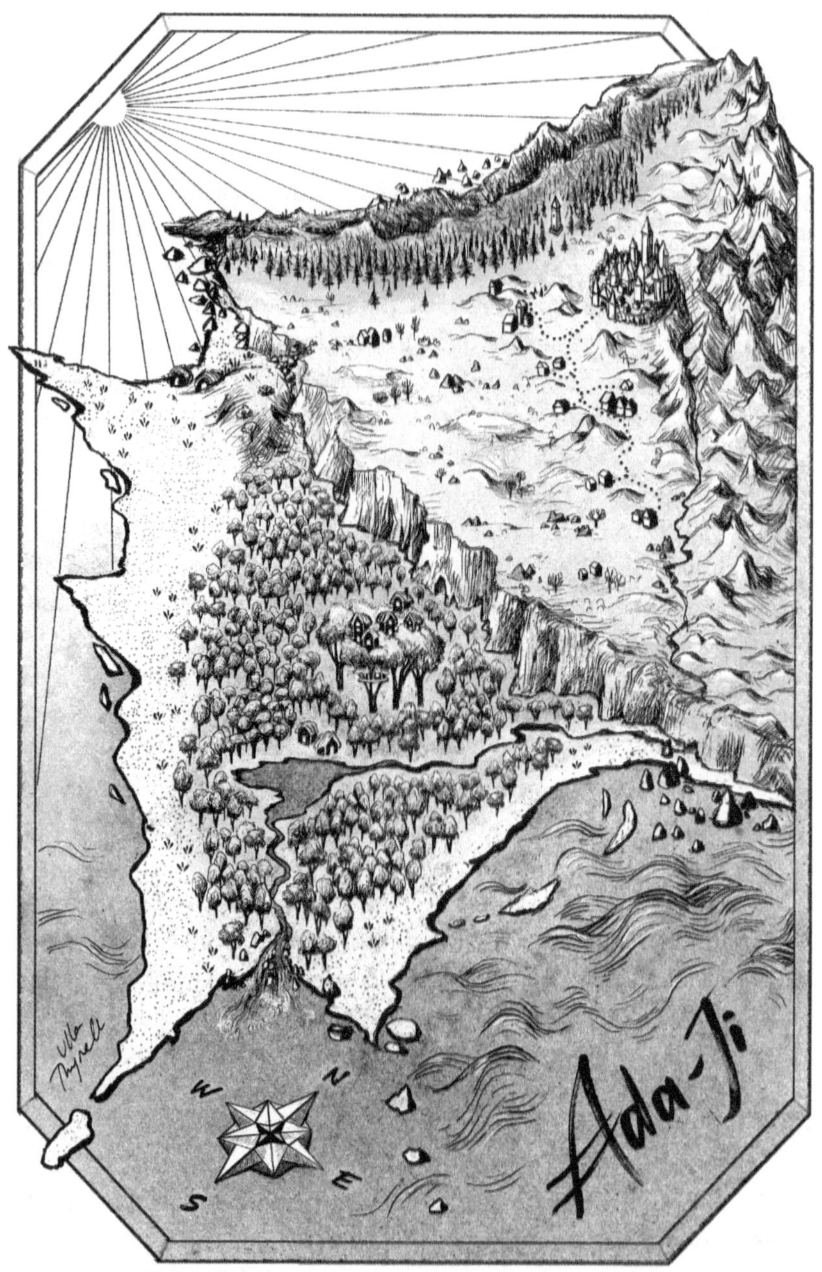

Ulla
Thynell
N
W
E
S
Ada-Ji

Rise

if I have harbored love inside my heart
it was for my friends

—Abū al-ʿAlāʾ al-Maʿarrī, from a ruba'i, c1000

Act 1

TIME

News used to be a matter of interest to Dime, but now that the world felt one stride from collapsing in every direction, her heart twitched at its mention. Ador sat down next to her, refilling his own cup with whatever was in the pitcher.

Dime tasted it. Like a berry tea, both sweet and bitter. Through the edges of the drawn curtains covering the windows of the high-class fairy's extra event space, the light looked like it was finally starting to dim. Dime wondered, this time, what Sol would see the next time ve rose.

"Dayn returned to Lodon," Ador started. "He's well, but concerned. There is much more to Ada-ji than we knew. Entire networks of tunnels, and even some hints that they were made or used during the Great War."

Yes, there were definitely tunnels, she thought, but said nothing, wanting to hear Ador's updates first before she bogged him down in their own developments. Her sense was that the tunnels were older than the Great War, and based on all she'd seen, she was starting to wonder even if the idea of one 'Great War' was far too simplified. If the Violence was good at anything, it was concealing its true nature.

"He's gone back to meet with the Construction Circle, to see what he can learn about the drilling efforts."

"They must be stopped as soon as possible," Dime muttered, the words slipping out. She closed her mouth, wanting again to hear what Ador had to say. It bore discordantly that she felt guilty sitting for a bell when others had operated with abandon for far too long. That they continued to do so. *Time*, she said under her breath.

That was always the thing, now. Even the urgency of Dayn needing to "learn" about the Boring Project was absurd—he was an expert on the huge CC drills and their use for geological research in the nor mountains. Yet they were drilling to the sur, near the Great Cliff, and Dime felt certain the diamond caves were the motivation for this. Finding them, destroying them—who knew. She'd tried twice to ask Sala to look into the rogue effort. Sala, who was the Light and thus in charge of everything, had no idea the drills had been moved. And thus if she didn't know about it, she doubted it happened. Dime rubbed her forehead.

"Yes, that's his goal," Ador continued. "I've got him tied into the Free Winds so we can get communications to each other." Ador stared at her. "He'll be glad that you're well, but seeing all of you now, I don't think he was worried enough." Standing off behind the table, Volana nodded slowly.

What did he mean by that? Dime glanced at Rock, Uchitar, and Luja. Rock's new clothes were already smudged and torn, but not so much to distract from the dirt on her neck and the tense pull of her mouth. Uchitar was trembling, his eyes unsteady. Scratches covered his hands and arms, and a bruise spread over the point of one cheekbone. There was a scuff across one of Luja's sleeves, a shirt ve'd picked up at the Underground that didn't quite suit ver. None of them looked like they'd slept. They really hadn't, not enough for a whole daytime to have gone by. Dime wondered if she looked as rough.

Her eyes caught Tum's, from her chair, where Agni was kneading her paws into Tum's arm. Her child grinned back, giving no indication of Dime's dishevelment. She always had Tum for that. Gratitude swelled.

"The Sol's Pillars are in full protest now," Ador continued. "Rallies, disruption of travel, confronting pyrsi and demanding their allegiance."

While he was keeping his tone level, Dime could hear the agitation in those last words. Batu had explained once to her that the Free Winds worked hard to break pyrsi from strict ideas of allegiance.

"Sala will have to do something soon," he said. "Pyrsi are scared, normal activities are halting, basic needs not being met because pyrsi are either out hollering, staying in their homes, or confronting the Pillars. There is no question it is the Violence, though not to the point yet of touch or physical harm. On top of that, she sent me a message."

"She?" Dime blurted out. "Sala?"

Ador nodded. "On a pyrsonal level, it suggested we should talk." He stopped, emotion clouding his eyes but only briefly. "Second, it held a note for you. But not from Sala," he quickly corrected. "From your friend, Zael. Dime, I'm sorry."

Dime hung her head.

"It was found in his room and turned into the Circles because it had your name on it. A name that caught some notice, so it made its way right to the top. Here." Ador held out a sealed fold of papers. His hand remained steady, but the note wavered a little as Dime took it.

> *To my friend, Dime.*

Definitely Zael's handwriting. . . . Handwriting of a pyr that no longer breathed. Sheets of paper waiting here in a world without him. She took a deep breath. She'd been through enough now, she could make it through this as well.

Everyone watched silently as she pried open the wax and unfolded the fine paper sheets. Not thinking about why, she began to read aloud.

> *Burgess Diamond –*
> *When you read this, my time will be over.*
> *Yours will not.*

> *I hope you're not upset that I gave back the item. It has been my experience working in circles of influence for a long time that while it is our sacred duty to give, trying to give away some things dissatisfies our burden for having received those things in the first place. Our threads in the fabric are not so easily torn. We cannot weave a better path if we deny the one that exists.*

The last few letters were hard to read, and the next paragraph was written at a different angle—each section was. As if he'd written the note over several sessions.

> *I miss you already. Not only you, of course, but you were kind enough to visit me, and I want you to know what that meant. I miss my most precious Yorm. I miss our children and their children. I miss the mail carrier, who sings as ve climbs the stairs. I miss my old coworkers. The tired Bakh that worked the deli. Sol. The rain. Everything.*

Dime was glad that Zael did not reference Yorm's coldness to Dime those last visits. He knew that she'd forgive his spouse. And she did. Not that she'd see her again. That was done.

> *Could you indulge me if I still think of you as Agent Dime? This does not subtract from the pyr you are now, but we had many cycles together and I would not want them erased. I have remembered a few moments of particular note. I'd like to share them, as I don't know if anyone else remembers these details. Sharing them . . . feels important.*

Zael proceeded to recall many of the concerts they'd seen, some of the issues he'd encountered working with the Circles, and times that Dime had strode into one office or another and cleared them up on his behalf. A time they'd laughed about an unfortunate typography error. Small details. Memories. A story about a tree that he liked and the animals who made it their home. A particular squip with a striped tail, who always moved close enough to be seen as Zael walked past. She stopped reading aloud and read the rest to herself. Then she saw the last lines of ink before the paper turned to blank.

May I indulge in poetry? One last time.

If I have now returned to memory, let me remain in yours.

Your friend, devoted scholar, and eternal flower-wielder –

Zael.

Postscript: I wish I had learned more about the fairies.

Dime refolded the papers and slid them into a pouch.

The group sat quietly. Luja's mouth was pressed closed as ve stared at the floor, not dissimilar to the way Ador had continued to gaze down as Dime read. Tum had wheeled over to the window, her back to the group. Uchitar was somewhere distant, lost in thought. Volana watched him intently. Only Rock caught her gaze. She gave her a tight little smile. It helped.

"Thanks for listening. He was a good friend."

That wasn't enough. It wasn't enough to say. A little pit dropped inside her, and she ignored it. She'd need time to consider his loss, his words, his stories. Time, right now, they didn't have.

"We've disrupted the Seats," she said. "Word of it is spreading. Another issue." She knew she should explain more, but she'd just lived it. She glanced over at Ador, hoping he'd understand. For now.

"Pito too, then," was all he said. "Hin is waiting for me at the Crossing. I hired a flier to take me here, and he wasn't ready for that yet." Dime could understand that.

Ador breathed in. "We had . . . words . . . after what happened. He wants to help. He apologized for how he treated you. I told him it wasn't just you; the fairies were part of this, and I could no longer spare the time to show him something he wasn't willing to learn on his own. He promised he understood."

Dime again took in Pyrilee's wide space, with clusters of soft seats, glossy sculptures, and artfully meandering marble counter-tops. Hin carried his troubled past from a small plains village, and she wondered if Ador, a pyr of reasonable wealth himself, had even considered this would not have been a great place to take the young pyr as an introduction to their common struggles. Fair or not.

The Crossing, on the other hand, was a place where pyrsi kept to themselves. Maybe spending some time there would help convey that pyrsi all just wanted to live their lives, contributing as they could along the way. It wasn't that complicated.

Frankly, she was not as bothered by Hin's treatment as she would have been just turns ago. Her recent experiences had caused her to place nearly everyone outside a thin shell, she'd come to realize. And so this pyr, who she'd really just met, had been behind that shell when he'd spoken in ignorance and haste. She would move on. Though she did not see them being close, they had a common goal. That was Dime's focus.

Volana had begun circling the table. Her wings flapped behind her, not as though flying but more the way a pyr might wring xyr hands. "Are you sure you don't need to rest?"

Rock and Dime met eyes. "We're sure," Rock said. "At least until we can tell pyrsi what we've seen, do something about it. There can't be rest. I will, however, compromise on one shower."

This place had so many water tanks, there were actually *eight* separate showers two levels down.

"I can agree to that," Dime said, not having enjoyed the film of the river water lingering on her skin over the past bells. The musk of the lower caves rested in her nostrils and she hoped to herself it would wash away. "Showers. Then what?"

"Let's go big," Rock said. Everyone turned to watch her.

"Let's get everyone together. You're in or you're in the dust at this point. Pito, Lodon, the Beds—any one of them could do something drastic any stride. We've got to get everyone together and put some sort of agreement on the table. A place to start. It won't happen until we get them together, eye-to-eye."

"Where?" she murmured, mostly still considering it.

"The Rise," Ador answered. "It's the largest meeting space at the Crossing. Easy to get to by toothcar or flight. Not really a secret. Not owned by anyone. It used to be a natural gathering area, but no one there likes to feel exposed, so over time they've covered it with canopies."

"Oh, right, the big tent," Rock said.

Ador's expression lifted just a little. "Sure. But it sounds much more ceremonious to call it the Rise. I propose we convince who we can and then we all meet there. We'll form a plan before the leaders arrive. Whoever we can get to assist."

"What is it?" Dime saw something else in his eyes.

"From what we've discussed . . . there's no time."

"I know," Dime said. Luja moved over to put vis arm around Ador, and he leaned in, with the look of not even an auncle, but a grandfather on his face. Were they so old? Or were they just feeling it?

"I propose first bell," Dime said. The others turned toward her, but no one responded. "It's easy to convey in both cultures. Easy to track. And it's symbolic. The Seats already convene at Sol's rise. Lodon doesn't attach shifts to Sol, but think of the ceremonies that take place at the advent of the light."

"I agree," Volana said, no longer pacing. "I worried a flap about tying this to Sol, when that speaks more to your land . . . yet it is our tradition." She glanced off, as if she'd never thought of the implications. One by one, everyone around the room nodded.

"It will be tight," Dime said. "As you know. Even with night-time just falling, we'll only have the entirety of half a turn to gather everyone."

"That will feel like forever given what we've seen," Luja said.

Having meant the opposite, Dime hoped that would be their issue.

"But you're all so tired," Volana said, scanning each of them like an inspector.

"We'll do what we have to," Dime said with more emphasis than she'd intended. Yet, the group showed no disagreement. Dime closed her eyes. She supposed this signaled that she was thinking.

The others respected the gesture, and when she opened them, they were watching her.

"With Volana's and Uchitar's permission, I will talk to Ferala. He knows me. We have . . . a connection."

"She's under arrest," Rock said, leaning back.

Dime shrugged. "Given that, I feel the one place the High Guards won't be looking for me is Chambers. Anyone who needs to rest can do so, here, while I'm gone. I promise, I'll come back."

"I'll come find you if you don't," Uchitar added, almost growling.

"I know you will," she said, smiling at him. "Just . . . give me a few bells. Spans," she corrected. "Spans."

Dime had recently told herself she would never go back into the Seats' complex—the thought made her whole body tense—but she could spare one more time. Once. She hoped.

Volana and Uchitar leaned in together and spoke softly. They turned back to the table.

"You have our blessing to approach the Seats, whether that is needed or not," Volana said. "I will notify the Foundry and ask each pyr who can for individual support: to witness the event, or to calm their neighborhoods when the news spreads. To prepare the burgesses. Uchitar will—"

"I'd like him to stay with me," Luja interrupted. "If he would. And Tum."

Volana paused, her lips parting in discomfort. Uchitar responded. "I would like that. I'll stay with Luja and Tum, and we'll make our way to the Crossing by land. We'll leave soon, as we'll be slower. I can't use valence the way that Dime does, but I can help Tum over any rough patches." He met Dime's gaze. "I will protect them."

Uchitar was wavering now, but soon he'd go through the worst of withdrawal. Could she subject her children to that? Dime looked at Luja, studying ver expression. "I agree." She turned back to Rock.

"Let me go with you," Rock stated, straightening.

Dime hesitated. "This time, I'd like to go alone. I think . . . I think maybe both of our strengths are needed right now. Our team."

Rock looked as though she were going to argue. But she didn't. "I'll power-nap; I'm really pro at it. Then I'll go home and contact DC. We could use their stability at the Rise."

She knew that contact wouldn't be easy for Rock. Rock's recent trials with the Intel Circle had just forced her out of Dawn's Circle, a shadow segment of the Ja-lal government dedicated to learning more about the fairies. But she was right—any solies with an understanding of Fo-ror culture and a willingness to connect should only help the gathering's chances. Dime started to say she'd see her when she got back, but she probably wouldn't. It was unlikely they'd cross paths again, at least not tonight. Rock would be there, at the Crossing. She knew she would.

"Hug?" Dime squeaked out.

"I'll see you in Sol's light," Rock said. The hug was light and fast. "I've got my gear," she said, her eyes downward. "No fliers or whatever, but I can catch rides once I get to the top. I'd better get going." Rock turned and left down the ramp, presumably for her shower or maybe the power nap. Even in a moment of melancholy, Dime had to smile. Only Rock would casually allude to climbing the Great Cliff after a quick nap. Dime realized she was still staring at the ramp, and she turned around.

"I'm well rested," Ador said, as if nothing had happened. "I'll leave right away to inform the Winds. I do have the means to call for fliers from here; they'll speed my way to the Crossing. There's a Free Winds post there—I can get Hin working with them on messages. Not just to attend, but to be more active in Lodon as well." He glanced off, as if debating with himself. "The Winds are normally talkers, but I know they're disturbed by the Pillars' rallies and growing interference. I can get them working to counter it. To dampen the effect."

It sounded like no one would be staying here. So she'd have no need to return. "If you'll meet me there," Dime said, thinking, "at the Crossing—we can fly together to Lodon. I can't risk getting our bench right now, but as long as you can borrow a seat for more than one, well, that's easiest." She pointed at the fairy-backed chairs. "One with good back support."

Ador acted like she'd asked him to pick up ripe avos at the grocer. "That will work fine," he said. "If you need to rest somewhere, I ask you to consider it. Even a bell or two might help."

"I'll consider it," she said. She was exhausted, but how could anyone rest, now? Knowing what was at stake.

Ador watched her a moment. "I see. Then it will be a long night."

Dime used valence to fly a sealed note to the stone arch.

> Seat Layanie,
>
> I am back and asking permission to enter. I must speak. With you both.
>
> Just eas of main entrance. I am nervous of unknown guards.
>
> D.

Two fairies arrived, yet she did not know them. "Like the rays of Sol," one whispered. With relief, Dime nodded.

They silently wrapped her in a huge black robe, and walked close by her side, guiding her through the now unguarded main entrance and then a series of empty passageways, difficult to see past the softly draping hood. She expected to arrive somewhere discreet. Layanie's office. An unmarked room. And so it was not expected when the hood was drawn back and she found herself standing in the center of the Chambers of the Seats, with its rounded dais and vaulted, curved ceiling.

One chair was empty.

Eight more were filled. High Seat Ferala looked like an elderly lyona, perched on his gem-embedded rest. Layanie poised on the edge of vis painted chair, observing calmly from Ferala's side. The others, she recognized but had not met, except for Dailawe, who curtly nodded. Dime waved her fingers, as Trowby had showed her. She looked for Tikinal but did not see him.

The guards left. All of them.

When she'd last stood before the Seats, the room had been alive with fairies bustling through the space: a host of workers, perhaps messengers and scribes. Now there were only nine: eight of the Seats and herself. The perfume she remembered had faded, leaving faint smells of cedar. With only one of the massive chandeliers lit, it felt as though she stood in a theater spotlight. Just herself and the distant rumble of the Circles' drills.

The complex had not collapsed; whatever Dime had done had energized the diamonds in the caves. The land stayed standing. For a while longer. Yet the drills continued. Though she was not using her valence, now that she had heard them, she could not stop hearing them. Everywhere, their rumble persisted in her consciousness, but here, it trembled deep in her bones. She was suddenly grateful that the War had not started already. That they were still able to talk.

It was nighttime, not the normal time for the Seats to convene. But of course, given all that had happened just spans before, they were here. Staring at her, silently.

She considered their inaction, even now. As glad as she was that they had not rushed to confrontation, what did it say that they sat, waiting? For whom did they wait?

"We are in great danger," she said.

Many of the Seats glanced awkwardly toward the center of the dais; Dime supposed there would normally be an introduction. Though it felt spurious now, she could not forget such things if she wanted their help.

"From you?" It was a Seat whose name she'd forgotten. Volana had told her about each of the Seats, but her thoughts were scattered and she didn't want to get it wrong. "Neimano has warned that you are dangerous; you will kill us on sight."

Her chest pulsed. Neimano's continued warping of the truth was a bright beacon of the Violence, yet his fellow leaders were so unfamiliar with malicious untruth that it flickered unperturbed around them, like a lightless fire.

"I don't know. I don't think so," Dime responded. "And I don't think you think so, if I'm here. I'll tell you what he meant, though. Because I survived the disease you called the curse, I carry some remnant within me." Blocking their reactions, she did not add that Neimano may have forced her body to contain more, as that was speculation. Nor did she add that the disease was known to spread easily and show itself quickly, as they would know that. "But I have lived many cycles close to others. And for several turns now, around fairies. No one has caught a thing."

They erupted in murmurs. Layanie raised vis hand, and the others quieted. Ve turned toward Ferala.

"I welcome Burgess Diamond of Lodon to speak," he said.

Dime paused. "Thank you, High Seat Ferala." She took a breath. "The vibrations you feel are caused by the Circles." She was sure they knew who the Circles were. "By large drills, meant for science. I do not think the Light ordered them to this region. I told her of the danger, but she is still figuring things out, as you would understand." She was still frustrated that Sala's inaction had allowed the drills to stay and then resume, but reminded herself that if they'd been off for a while, then it would have been harder for Sala to find evidence of them. The argument didn't quite convince her, and she heard the tension in her next words.

"I know the magnitude of what this has done, and still could do. If you would be angry with the Circles, then know that what Neimano has done and has tried to do is nearly unspeakable. Yet. Nothing is unspeakable if it could be prevented from happening again."

Then she stopped. The Seats had talked about Neimano. How much, she didn't know. But she saw in their eyes. She saw the empty chair. His odd behavior could likely no longer be overlooked. She wouldn't belabor it, not if they had a sense. As long as they would move forward for now. Other consequences would not be hers to give.

"We must act now. Pito is unstable, literally as well as the whispers in its . . . branches." She'd been about to say streets; she hoped the replacement worked. "Lodon is unstable, with shouting rallies and teetering peace. It is only a matter of time before one side marches on the other with the Violence not out of mind."

She was surprised that no one reacted. It was as though they were afraid to react, afraid to betray their feelings or react incorrectly. Each waiting to see what the others would do. Dime grimaced.

"I have learned—and it has taken me too long to learn this—that our fears are stoked by our inequities. They are intertwined, and so the solution cannot only be with each other, but within ourselves. It's time for a new age. A new age where old ills are acknowledged, corrected as they can be, and then left behind. A new age where current imbalances are let go. The world will never be fair, will it? But we are not helpless. Only if we let our imbalances go, only then will we rise."

She took a breath. They were really letting her have this. "I believe I can get the Light to a meeting if I have your word you will attend. We will meet at the Crossing, at the first light of the next daytime. A group of us will draft basic terms, for your mutual consideration and to form the basis of a potential first agreement. A way to move forward and prevent this imminent collapse." She was careful not to reference Sol. She assumed they knew of the Crossing, but if they didn't, there were many who could tell them.

"And in case it is not apparent, keep Neimano under observation. By Seats or by High Guards that you individually trust. Ensure he does not intervene and does nothing of harm."

A Seat on the end turned hard enough that xyr heavy chair grated on the dais. "Follow a *Seat*?" Xe waved an arm toward the empty chair. "He is not here, but he has not had his say. And who is she to speak so?"

Ah, then they hadn't fully talked about it. Layanie knew Neimano's nature. She remained sure of that.

"Neimano is a traitor," Ferala stated. "She is his victim."

A wave of intense heat rushed into her face. She dared not look at him.

He was met with silence.

"I will tell you the rest when Burgess Diamond departs. She should not have to hear it. Not again."

Dime gave him a slight bow. "Then you will be there?"

Ferala clasped his hands together and closed his eyes. "I will."

As Dime left, the soft cloak swirling back around her, the chamber burst into shouts.

Dime did not pause to rest, but headed right to the Crossing in Pyrilee's chair. He wouldn't want the piece returned after it had been scratched through a few of Dime's landings anyway.

Fairy chairs never had the support Dime wanted; it had at least amused her to find this one with a stone inlay suggesting the octahedral shape of a diamond on the back. Given that her last entrance into the Crossing had been in an ill-fitting suit and frumpy hood, she figured this one would be in a little more style.

She would have kept the secretive robe on—she felt rather cool in it—but she had to strap her bag to her front and she didn't want to look like a flying chunk of soot. She did work the rolled robe into her bag. Though the large backpack never liked being overstuffed, maybe the cloak would serve as a good pajama gown on chilly turns. As long as no one in Lodon saw her wearing its hood. As she was absolutely going to do.

The Crossing, what was visible in the nightlight, looked larger from the sky than she remembered from the ground. A round, dusty basin where the Great Cliff dwindled to a pass, it qualified at least as a village, full of small structures and canopies dotted prudently with exterior lights. Unlike a normal village, with pyrsi milling about, pyrsi here tended not to spend a lot of time outside, using the modest paths only to enter, exit, or traverse the mostly windowless tents, sheds, and buildings. Only one pyr was visible, a fairy, who flapped his wings in what looked to Dime like a large jump, landing just short of a small awning before disappearing from view.

Up on the hillside, she saw something she hadn't seen walking through on the main road: a series of draped cloths and canvases, like roof panels, working their way up a gentle section of the basin's slope.

That must be the Rise, she presumed.

Remembering what she'd seen here as the protocol, she landed in middle area of the road to state her intent. Where to land was clear—there was a large oval of well-trodden ground, which now with more awareness, she saw was broadly visible to the small town, as if few built a structure that didn't have some view of the arrival area. Not sure if she was supposed to yell out "free high-end chair with scratches on it" or something, she stood, slinging her backpack on. She glanced around at the varied structures and small, shuttered windows.

"Is Ador here?" she called out, feeling a bit awkward. So much for looking cool.

That said, no one rushed to accost her or to demand to know her business. At the Crossing, apparently a pyr's business was still xyr own. Dime smiled. Even knowing that inside the shrouded tents and structures, pyrsi were undoubtedly peering out and murmuring, for a stride she was alone on the dusty path and this felt just about right.

Luckily, she didn't have to holler twice. Ador came striding out, Hin trailing behind.

Ador briefly reached for her hands, relief in his eyes. Glad, she supposed, that she'd returned from the complex.

"I'm sorry for how I treated you." Hin stumbled over his words. "I am learning about the fairies."

"We're all learning," Dime said. "I know I've learned so much since this all began." The sting of his reaction hadn't left her, but she had other issues on her mind and couldn't take it on right now.

"I knew you'd pick that one," Ador said, pointing at the chair's stone inlay.

"Think you could get it delivered to Volana's?" Dime asked, the idea suddenly occurring to her. "I owe her a chair."

"I can definitely do that. Hin, could you put this back with our things?"

Hin seemed happy enough to oblige, and he hefted the chair up and walked back toward one of the taller buildings.

Ador raised his eyebrows.

"Oh, right. They agreed to come here. At least, Ferala did. The High Seat."

His mouth hung open briefly. "Alright then, off to find Sala. But first, I have a surprise for you," he said with a smile.

The last time Ador had a surprise for her, things had gone a bit askew, but she didn't bring that up, as proud as he seemed of whatever he was about to show her.

As they walked back up to a building, she saw it herself. Though shielded from the dust by a cloth cover, she recognized the legs poking out. "Rosebench!" Dime said, hastening her steps. Harm it all, she was more than a little happy to see that bench.

"You know, we got that less than a turn ago," she noted. "But I'm attached."

"Love at first sight," Ador said. "I was the same with my recliner." His expression shifted. "We're going to Lodon? Do you need anything here first?"

"I'd rather just go," she said. "We'll be back soon enough." She glanced toward the bench. "You can't be ready for this."

Ador chuckled, perhaps nervously, as Dime uncovered the padded bench, set her big, bulky bag next to Ador's sleek messenger-style bag, and they sat on either side. She noticed he was already gripping the rope handle, so with a quick warning that this was it but no ceremony, they lifted into the night. Ador let out a long whistle as they moved up and quickly into Sol's Reach.

"This can't be stranger than being flown on a blanket by fairies," Dime offered.

"Each has their charm. But when our ordeals have passed a bit, I do look forward to a stint at home."

"In your recliner," Dime added.

"Yes," he confirmed.

They'd taken turns telling stories to help keep Dime alert over the long flight to Lodon. She'd tried not to think about the time or distance, though she certainly felt it when the bench finally approached the Circles' complex. Certain the skies would be watched anyway, she made no effort to hide as she flew in, not landing on the balcony near Sala's office this time, but closer to the atrium.

Guards stood ready as they opened the door, following Ador and Dime as they climbed the stairs toward Sala's office.

She was waiting at her desk.

It was clear Ador had never been inside the Light's pyrsonal office—he was unable to conceal his awe at the circular room, the lights of the city twinkling below through wide swaths of beveled windows, tallest to the wes, and muted to the nor and eas where the dark shapes of the mountains painted jagged lines against the night sky. Yet he couldn't spare a long look, as Sala walked toward them, her face solemn but a mix of emotions in her eyes.

"Ador," she said, faltering briefly. Dime understood. Ador had only looked statelier and more handsome with age.

"It's so good to see you again," he replied. "I'm sorry that we're here on business. Perhaps another turn."

Sala looked more tired than before. To the extent she made no effort at a show. "I'm ready," was all she said.

I hope you are, Dime thought. "The drilling has resumed, Light Sala. It's causing reverberations through the area near the Seats' complex, an area that is already riddled with tunnels and so the impacts are amplified. There was almost a collapse within the complex itself, but it was prevented. For now. Actions by others likely factored in, but to be clear—the CC drills have already caused irreparable damage, and will cause catastrophic damage if they are not stopped."

Dime didn't wait for her reaction. "We are out of time. As you know, Sol's Pillars are marching through the streets of Lodon, disrupting peace, life, and economy. Jaza is holding rallies, frightening burgesses, urging that fairies will invade their homes. I just left the Chambers of the Seats, listening to them shout at each other in disarray. The workers in the complex, they'll hear. Pito will know of this soon, and then the whole forest. It's only a matter of time until one of them flies here, or someone here travels there. It's time. It's time to make a choice."

"It's an impossible choice," she snapped back. "We've discussed this. How casually you ask me to involve the fairies—a pyrsi I've never even met—without knowing the potential consequence." Dime hadn't brought up working with the fairies, but Sala knew that was her intent.

"You've met *me*, Sala. Sure, I know I'm one of us. But I was born there. I now have friends there. You know me. And if not well enough, Ador knows me. Would he stand here with me if he thought our actions would truly bring harm?"

"It's such a risk." Sala walked to face the wesside windows.

"Yes, but it's a risk either way. There isn't any more waiting it out. You know that. You see it. If you do nothing, what will happen? Will the Sol's Pillars declare their rule? They are calling Jaza 'the Light.' Did you know that?"

Sala's hands clenched. *Ah.* She did know that. "High Seat Ferala has agreed to meet at the Crossing at first bell, with the hope that you will be there also. I have only told him what I will now tell you:

Ador and I, and a fairy we trust, intend to draft some basic terms, in order to codify a first agreement: an intent to work together. Give us an avenue for discussion."

"If you think so poorly of me, what will I have to do with it?"

"You don't know what I think," Dime continued, noting that Ador stood silently, letting her talk, as Sala stared out at the city. "And you are the Light. Pyrsi know you. However you feel about it, they revere you. To throw away that sort of influence in this critical moment would be a terrible mistake. That's my view. We need you there. We need pyrsi spreading the word that you were there, that you stood face-to-face with Ferala. That you took the bridge. That if their leaders can meet and listen, maybe others can too. Please. Give us that start. That chance."

Dime glanced around, to the golden desk. The tall lamps. The glass artpiece. A ring of chairs. She wasn't saying it right. These were supposed to be moments for grand speeches, and all she could think of, now that she was here, were practical sentiments and plain words. Then, Ador spoke. Only in a soft voice.

"Sala, please."

Dime closed her mouth and stepped forward to stand next to Ador. Together, they waited, as Sala stood, the shape of her thickly padded shoulders unmoving between the golden cast of the lamps and the lights of the city beyond.

"I'll try it," she finally said, turning around. "But if my presence is really to be a part of this, let me do it properly. A delegation. The banners of Sol's Reach. The Light, as she should be. I will be there."

"First bell," Ador repeated.

"I'll be there," Sala said.

Dime had wanted to insist that the drilling be addressed, but Ador's gestures had stopped her.

"It won't matter," he said, as they walked, uninterrupted, through the dark atrium. "I know that look. She thinks you're mistaken on the drills. Or perhaps she can't accept that the CC is lying to her. The Violence within her own ranks—that's a big adjustment. She's going to the meeting; it's the symbolism we need. We'll deal with the drills ourselves."

"How?" Dime tried to think through the clouds in her mind.

"My love, your spouse has been spending bells working the CC for intel. We'll ask his advice."

Dayn! That's right; he was in the city. She was getting so tired, she could hardly keep it all straight. She yearned to hold him close.

"This is going to crowd our deck," Ador noted, as Rosebench flew off toward his tower.

A swirl of pink with sparkling brass accents greeted them at the outside door, along with the soft scent of clovebulbs. Batu leaned in for quick hugs before scanning them both. "Oh, you look so tired. Don't hesitate to go right to sleep."

Dime could almost hear Rock's carved owl calling to her from the guest room's bedtable. "I'll take some brew instead," she said, stepping in through the door.

Her tiredness was pushed aside as she saw Dayn waiting in the living space. Though always a familiar sight, after what she'd been through since leaving the Underground, he felt a bit unreal, standing in front of Batu's couch. He was real. He was there. She put the knot aside for one stride and instead enveloped him in as tight of a hug as she could muster. She felt his cheek against hers, then he moved away.

"I can't quite hug you around this bag," he said with a chuckle.

"Ah, right." Together, they lowered it off to the side.

Dayn stared down at it a long moment. "That bag is aging faster than I am."

Dime wasn't sure what he meant until she gave the bag a look. He had a point. When Ella had made it for her, back before her first intentional trip to the Heartland, it had been clean, sturdy, and stood tall like the most dedicated worker. Now, it was torn, scuffed, stained, and bore the unmistakable ripples of having been submerged in lake water.

"It's a really good bag," was all she could say. It felt very odd, just the two of them together. Ador must have told him, but still. "We are not terrific at supervising our children, either?"

"But they're independent?" he tried.

"I think that counts," Batu said firmly, bringing in a tray of brew. "I already had some cooking," she explained.

"I asked her to make some," Dayn said. "Perhaps I thought it the most reliable way to summon you."

"It worked!" She threw up an arm.

They sat together on the sofa. Dime felt it surreal—surreal only in its innate familiarity in the face of nothing normal at all.

"Has Rock been here?" she asked.

Dayn shook his head. "Haven't seen her. Is Hin with you?"

"No," Ador answered. "He's at the Crossing, and knows I'll be back. I admit once I saw the size of Dime's flying sofa, I decided not to invite anyone else."

Dime would have smiled, but too much was on her mind. "I'm sorry to cut to it," she said, "but we've got to stop the drills. Ador and I are putting a meeting together; he thought you could help with the drills."

He nodded. "Turns out, they weren't operating for a while. I don't know what's going on to the nor, I'm only talking about the ones they moved sur," he clarified. "I'm wondering if they actually hit a few of the diamonds. I would think hitting them directly could damage the equipment."

She decided not to get into her theory that she'd broken the drills with her valence. From afar. Wasn't really the point. "They're running now," she said. "They are very close to points of vulnerability, and the whole complex is at risk." Again, she decided to leave out that she'd stopped a major collapse. "And if the complex is at risk, the city's at risk, peace is at risk, and all of Ada-ji is at risk."

Dayn grimaced. "I could tell the equipment was still operating, but not being able to fly, I'm limited in the ability to travel and search. I decided my time was best spent getting back here. Getting whatever information I could. The CC is full of good pyrsi. You know that. Pyrsi I knew would not want to be faced with my word that they were putting pyrsi in harm's way.

"Either way, I've learned where the drills are, and I have enough of a feeling that it's just as we suspected. Someone in the Circles is trying to get to the diamonds, but because of my association with you, I can't get further than that."

His head shot up. "That sounded wrong."

"No, I understand." She raised a hand. "*My* association with me has been the same way. Anyway, does it matter?"

"What?"

"Their intent. Whoever's doing this. They're acting with such recklessness I don't know if I even care why." She tapped the seat. "If you've got the location, let's go ask them to stop."

"They might say no." Dayn noted. There was something off in his tone.

"We can talk about it on the way." She could walk Dayn through her thoughts on the Violence, and the boundaries between one pyr and another, and the difficulties of risk and uncertainty, but the fact was—even if there wasn't always an easy choice, no action *was* a choice. She wished that it were easy.

And she couldn't avoid the knot.

"There's one more thing." She glanced at Ador, but he didn't react. With a breath, she addressed the room. "As Dayn knows, when I was a ba'pyr, I survived a terrible disease. According to Luja, some amount of this disease—ve called it an . . . interferer—could linger in a pyr's system, but the body has learned to block it. In my case, it's possible I was even injected with more, to create a stronger concentration."

Ador tightened his expression, while Batu somehow managed to look like she was listening to the wind. Dayn drew a slow breath. Dime watched him with worry.

"He intended to give us a substance that could revive this disease in our bodies and spread it to others. At least, it was his backup plan if at least one of us didn't turn Fo-ror spy. Anyway. The fairies, they called it the curse. I likely still have this substance inside me."

"Since you were a ba'pyr?" Dayn's brow wrinkled.

"Yes."

"And Luja knows about this?"

"Yes."

"Did ve tell you to stop it?" Now he sounded angry.

Dime tried to remember. Actually. "Yeah. Ve did."

"Good. Here's the thing. I am tired of this fairy getting involved in our lives. If you need additional medical care, we'll make sure you get it. Everyone has needs. Everyone is different. We take care of each other. But, what, does everyone who's ever been sick have to go around warning pyrsi? Anyone who's survived trauma? Anyone who's been near another pyr that day who might have had some-thing? Anyone who doesn't know if their food was properly cleaned? Anyone who might stumble and knock something over?"

Dime hadn't seen him this upset. And he wasn't done.

"You would never put pyrsi at undue risk. We're all a risk. Everything is a risk. The only curse I couldn't bear would be knowing you were out there and I couldn't be next to you. The rest, we'll figure out." He sat back, not even meeting Dime's eyes. She longed to embrace him.

Ador cleared his throat. "We're getting the leaders together at first bell. Fo-ror and Ja-lal." Dayn uncrossed his arms, and Batu spun back, dropping her neutral expression. While *the leaders* could mean many things, when Ador said it, it was clear he wasn't referring to just anyone.

"I need to talk to some of the Free Winds and come up with a plan," he continued. "There are some prominent pyrsi whose presence would help. Either to calm or to witness, I want to get them there." He rubbed his chin. "It'll help with their investment. Batu, you're welcome to accompany me to the Crossing; we'll take one of the Winds' cars. I'll get driving help. Several pyrsi I know would love to see this.

"Dime and Dayn, why don't you go on ahead and meet up with Hin and the others." A grin escaped him. "Dayn, the flying sofa is lovely. I think you'll quite enjoy it. No need to stop at Ella's," he added, turning to Dime. "I sent her a note."

Oh. Good. She'd thought of Ella but was worried about taking the time right now to alert her. Of course Ador could get her a note—a car, too, if she'd accept it. But about the flying. "Um," Dime started. "Do you mind if I borrow one of the Free Winds' cars also? A larger one?" She'd like to have room to transport her whole family back, wherever 'back' ended up being. It would take longer, but then she could think about what to write on the way without having to concentrate on flying. Or truly, she didn't want to subject the lovely Rosebench to the chalky dust of the Crossing. Rock would get a place somewhere, and she'd have a nice furnishing to start with. Maybe someday they'd enjoy a coco moss together on Rosebench and not worry about flying and hiding and other nonsense.

"No issue at all," Batu answered. "Dayn, Alur will have one ready."

Dayn turned to Dime. "That won't take me long. I'll return with the car. You finish that brew, and we'll be on our way." He gave her a pointed look, which to outside eyes might appear to be a look of longing, but Dime knew what he was signaling. The drills. They could go there on the way. She nodded.

After Dayn left, Dime turned to her friends. "I'm going to try drafting the agreement. I mean, why not me? I've seen both societies lately; not many can say that." No one was equipped to do this, so she was mostly convincing herself. But it was true she'd seen both recently. Even in the Underground, cultural senses had shifted, having such rare contact with either society outside of their stone walls.

"I've also been collecting notes from my conversations with both of you and with Volana. I wrote a list of interests in the spirit of some generic coalition, but nothing congealed. Now, I'm thinking. What about a more concrete agreement? A setting of more specific expectations? It will at least give us all a place to start. I just . . . don't think we have time anymore for a slower approach. No, that's not right," she corrected. "We will do the slower approach. But we need something more substantive to make it feel real. To solidify participation. Something that ends the imminent threat. Sets further talks in place. Anyway. When you get there, would you review what I have?"

"We'd be happy to," Batu said, with Ador nodding, his eyes lighting a bit.

"And once Volana arrives, I can get her take. And anyone else either of you recommend."

"Aren't you excited?" Batu asked, her voice raised with intensity.

"I don't know." She looked up. "Depends how it goes. I've lost . . . faith."

"Don't," Batu said.

Dime tried to smile politely. She hoped it didn't come off patronizing.

"Please. I'm not saying it to be naïve. We can't lose faith in the world. Not when the world may need us most."

Writing in a car was *not at all pleasant*, but time was passing, and Dime was going to get this thing done. Not only did Alur have a car ready, she'd found someone eager to drive them there. As Ador had indicated, there were many Free Winds thrilled at the idea of seeing the Crossing themselves—talking to "real fairies." While many of them wouldn't have risked it with the Circles before, perhaps they felt the shift in the air.

Situated in the back row, at least Dime didn't need to pedal. She saved her own energy—and also not wanting to scare the eager Aoch who pedaled along with Dayn—by not using valence to help move the car along. Not to say she couldn't swing a small flying-car episode, but well, she was trying to write. Dime did light a glowstone, but the Aoch couldn't see it wasn't just a small lamp on the bag hook. Besides, she continued to chatter at Dayn, something he dealt with politely.

Dayn and Dime had both tried to warn the young driver before they left that they had a stop to make that the Circles might not appreciate, but she'd not really wanted to hear it, so they finally relented and just got in the car.

Turned out, Dime really had forgotten how bumpy toothcars could be, especially outside of the city.

It was hard enough keeping the loose papers clipped together, and on top of that, she'd grabbed the largest pad Batu had, which ended up holding some rather epically large paper. Even the Circles didn't use this large of paper, outside of banners or maps. Actually, the Circles used the same, smaller notepads in most of their offices. After side-eying the unusual stack for a stride, she'd quickly embraced the idea; the huge sheets would certainly have a greater effect if they actually got pyrsi to sign them. Definitely frameable.

While she'd wait on *that* version until she could sit at a table that wasn't moving, she wobbled back and forth as the teeth of the eight wheels dug into the stony land and they moved across the night, the rhythm of the turning gears clanking on.

She started with a list of things that both cultures would have to do, if there was any chance of working together. Realizing the length of the list would likely be prohibitive, she crossed out the ones that weren't imminently critical. This wasn't easy. Issues could be important, but in many cases, they might be better held for a longer discussion. She also needed the agreement to feel balanced: similar concessions for each. Except the issues each held were unique. She rubbed her head, realizing no matter what she selected and didn't select, someone would take issue with her choices.

A few times, she drooped down toward the paper, her eyes weighting shut. Foreseeing this, Batu had given her cold brew in a flask, which turned out to be rather concentrated. Grateful, she took another sip.

Even the Aoch's chatter slowed after a while, and then a new sensation emerged. A pulsing in her fingers and a drumming in her ears. The drills.

She saw no looming shapes across the dimly-lit plains. That didn't make sense.

With a word to the driver, Dayn stopped pedaling and the car slowed to a halt.

He turned back to Dime, raising his voice. "They dug a trench for them, so it's hard to see what's going on unless you're right there. Fairies could fly above, but the Circles know the fairies don't fly into Sol's Reach, just as they obviously felt the Great Cliff an uncrossable line. At least that used to be the case. Once your visitors disillusioned them of having boundaries or time, they accelerated the effort. It's why they're so brash now."

He stopped. "That's an important note. They were going to do this before. It was already in work."

Dime would need to think about that later.

"I learned a lot when I was back in the office," he continued. "Enough that I hope we'll be able to prove who did this, and then we can start to understand why. For now . . . even if I get them to turn the drills off, I don't think we can risk someone turning them back on when we leave. Not with everything at stake. Dime?"

She thought she understood. It would be critical to keep them turned off, as recently as she'd stayed a disaster, and with the meeting upcoming. He meant to disable them, somehow, and she couldn't disagree. She was so tired of all this. Tired of unwinnable choices and damaging and weight. Always pulling at her, always something else. She tried to collect herself, reminding herself what she'd thought before. Stopping the drills without consent would be the Violence. Letting the drills be turned back on was also the Violence, as she now understood. She still knew that the Violence *could* be categorically wrong, but as one line after another had crumbled like chalk—like they had always been chalk—their choices grew much more difficult. The Violence was now a thorn that could be grabbed, not an evil lurking behind a veil.

"I understand, Dayn. They're the ones doing this. Not us." He had, of course, not heard her thoughts.

Dayn nodded to his co-driver. "You're sure?" He made it sound like they'd discussed it further, or some version.

She nodded with vigor.

"Dime?"

"I trust you," she said, repeating it, as her voice at first was too soft over the humming and grating of metal, even at a distance.

"Then let's go. Carefully," he said to the driver.

Dime considered the unmarked dropoff ahead. "I can help," she offered. "Start pedaling. I'll tell you when to stop." Closing her eyes, she reached out with valence, immediately feeling where the land called out in agony.

She understood something she hadn't before. The agony wasn't the change. It was the spirit. Land could be dug, moved, built upon, grown on—in the service of life, happiness, and peace. Mountains could grow and mountains could fall. But the moment pyrsi put those things at risk without thoughts of balance, the land cried out.

With valence, a pyr could hear it.

"A little more," Dime said, as the car ground along. Yes, it was a large trench, enough to fit a few smaller Lodon towers, and the road down was on the opposite side. She reached forward to get the Aoch's attention. What had she said her name was? Dime had written it down. Oh, right, *Fe'Ita*.

"Ita, I have the ability to use valence. Like . . . fairies do. Do you mind if I lift the car in? To make us fly?"

"Are you serious?" she said, setting an elbow up on the seat. She stared back at Dime. "I mean, yeah. Go!"

"I've never been so serious," Dime answered, a little energy returning as she lifted the car up and into the trench. Not wanting to risk pyrsi seeing the car lowering in, she added no light, but reached out with valence to sense the shape of the rock and the metal platforms within it. An area had been flattened on this side of the trench, surrounded by huge crates, and she moved them toward its center. As they lowered, the sounds of the tall, orange-painted drills pounded in her ears and chest and limbs, and their piercing, forceful shapes formed in her vision against a series of industrial lamps below.

She also saw the anger in Dayn's eyes, and she remembered the anger she'd first felt when she realized what the Circles were doing. Now, was that anger dulled simply because she already knew it was going on? Perhaps it was her exhaustion, or her mind trying to protect her, but the thought was distressing, nonetheless. She set the car down, doing her best to gentle the landing. Dayn lit the car's main lamp.

"Hey!" voices called from a metal path around the three drills, as pyrsi ran toward the car and Ita hissed in excitement.

Dayn ran in front of the car, waving his CC badge as the pyrsi reached them. "Ma'Dayn, CC. I need to talk to the site manager."

"You have no authority here," a pyr said.

"Who does?"

No one answered.

"What is going on here?"

No one answered.

Dayn held his badge higher. "I'd like to talk to whoever is in charge at this site. I have senior standing in the CC and I have pyrsonally confirmed that first, these drills are not authorized to be here, and two, they've caused damage from here all the way to the gorge, evidence of which is sitting at the Towers right now. I intend to disable the drills until a full CC investigation can be completed. You can help me or I can urge you to leave for your safety."

"We aren't touching anything," a pyr said, though xyr voice was less certain.

"I am. Last chance to help," Dayn warned.

The pyr turned xyr back and walked away.

Dayn looked back at Dime. "Good news is, I've actually been able to rest. And Batu's brew: not *quite* as good as Ella's but definitely contains more pep." He grinned. "Luja taught me something, and Tum got me practicing. Now, are you ready? I could use your help making sure no one gets hurt."

Dime could not fathom what he was going to do, but she tried to clear her mind, wrapping one hand around her diamond. It felt cool against her shaking hand.

Dayn marched over to the metal platforms where pyrsi were filing out of a series of small control sheds, craning to see the visitor, perhaps even hoping to stop him. Dime could see him, clear within the bright lights surrounding the machinery. Walking right through the group of workers, Dayn placed his hands against the base of one of the drills, leaning forward like one of his upper back stretches. The outer casing for the moving bit started to creak, with a loud screeching noise. Steam started to gather around him and the screech grew to a higher pitch. She worried that the steam looked hot, as all the others were backing away. Dime suddenly felt the pendant vibrating against her hand and chest. It was helping him. How was that possible?

"Cut the engines! Cut them!" someone yelled, as the shaft bent and folded like a loop-pin, pointing down into the trench. As pyrsi ran around and Dayn strode to the next drill, Dime worried someone might justify harm against him, so she directed a barrier and watched, as Dayn bent the towering shafts of other now-stopped devices. Then, perhaps gratuitously, he pushed one of the larger intact pieces over, as Dime verified no one was in its way.

It fell down into the rough-hewn border of the trench with a big, squeaky creak and then a loudly echoing clatter.

Noting the pyrsi slowly walking backward, Dime let Dayn's barrier drop.

"You ok?" Dime asked Ita, staring from the car's front row. She nodded, sort of, her mouth hanging open.

"So it turns out," Dime said to the gaping driver, "Ja-lal have valence too."

"So much strength," Ita murmured. "So much."

Dayn faced the group, bellowing with unnatural force, enough that she could hear him clearly. "Oh, for your reports. Ma'Dayn of Lodon. Dee. A. Wye. En. Badge number One Five Eight Four Four."

Brushing his hands together, he walked toward their toothcar and got back in. The door clicked shut. "Might want to get us out of here."

Still considering all of this but agreeing it was awkward to stay, Dime lifted the car back into the night, taking the extra effort to set them fully out of view.

"You're going to be fired from the Boring Project," she noted.

"Can I help with your music school? I'll raise funds so we can offer free lessons."

"Maybe we get some of these fairy ideas involved, we won't have to. Some," she repeated, chuckling a bit.

"Was that . . . the Violence?" Ita asked, her voice shaking.

Dayn looked to the younger pyr. "That's your decision to make, but for me, I consider that fully authorized CC maintenance activity."

Ita didn't look so sure, and Dime felt glad she wasn't. Dayn spoke calmly to her and slowly, they rolled off again, using the pedals. But the truth was, her own unplanned use of valence had taken energy Dime didn't have, and so she struggled, now, even to focus on the paper. On her notes. Resting for a stride, she stared out at the silhouettes of trees and land formations against the sky.

She'd never appreciated how many colors the night held. Sol, sure—the rising and setting of bright light against Lodon's golden towers was a thing of legend, fit even for her father's stories. The night held just as many.

One just had to settle into it more. Blues, indigoes, blacks, and deep greens, spattered with a rainbow of muted lights. The colors reminded her of fairy wings. Maybe Dime didn't need wings. She only needed the night.

Dayn murmured something to Ita, and again, the car stopped. "I'm sorry," Dayn said. "I'm feeling disoriented, and my legs are shaking."

Now that the drills had been taken from ops, maybe it was best they took a break. Surely Ita could use one as well.

"We have time," he said, but it was more of a question.

Ita had recently slept, so she decided to read a book by Dime's light in the car—the source of which she did not question—and Dayn and Dime tried to stomp the dirt into a flat enough space for a small rest.

"Sorry, I had a blanket," Dime said, "but I flew it away to distract pyrsi from noticing me. It was Batu's, too."

"Yeah, right now I don't think I need a blanket to sleep. How do you do all that? And keep going?"

"I wish I didn't have to," Dime answered. "Now, rest well. She'll be over here before you know it."

"Any chance she'll leave?"

Dime remembered Ita's face as Dayn had single-handedly bent poles of metal that had taken dozens of metalworkers to cast. "No."

Ita did not leave, and she looked guilty as she tapped them awake. Dime groaned.

She never liked those short sleeps where she somehow awoke

more tired, more groggy, and more drained than before, but she hoped in some way it had helped her. Dayn seemed to have regained some strength, or perhaps he was pretending as much as she was.

Dayn insisted on pedaling again, and when her diamond buzzed a little, she realized he was getting some help. This didn't seem to affect her, not in any way she could detect. She felt for the valence and brushed against a tiny thread, familiar but also different. When Dime had unknowingly used valence to drive the car, she'd been moving the pedals. Yet, Dayn's energy flowed within his legs themselves. She didn't think he knew he was doing it, but that could be a conversation for another day. Ita didn't seem to notice.

"Shouldn't there be a road?" Dayn asked. It had been rather bumpy.

"Of course there should," Dime answered, not having meant for it to sound so snippy. She softened her tone. "Pyrsi aren't really supposed to go here—since we don't admit it exists—so they come in from a few different angles. Yes, I know, you can only draw one line between Lodon and the Crossing but travelers usually pick a sur village to start from and then vary it a bit. Anyway, the path on this side almost doesn't form until the village itself."

From his silence, Dime had a feeling he was considering the term *village*. "I don't know what to call it," she said. "More like a market district without a city? But pyrsi live there?"

"I'm excited to see it," Ita said. "I know it's real. I know pyrsi who have been there." Dime was relieved the young pyr was not uncomfortable staying with them, especially seeing them both use valence. In contrast, she grew more animated as they drove, chattering about her work with the Free Winds, and her thoughts about the Crossing.

"Ita?" Dime started. "I'm glad you were here with us, for this drive. I suggest we will all remember it. I need you to know, I don't know what will happen when we get there. It could be the beginning of the end, the beginning of the beginning, or some mess I can't imagine. But I liked meeting you, and I'm glad we were here together tonight."

"Wherever 'here' is," she responded.

Dime laughed. That was a good point. They'd covered a good bit of ground. And, er, trench.

Unlike the looming lights of a normal village, there was very little to guide them other than a dip in the shadow of the land against the horizon. Almost out of nowhere, the walls of the basin rose to each side, and their pedaling smoothed over a packed-down road, with the shapes of the Crossing's small buildings gathered primarily to one side of the path, a spotty mix of lamps and glowstones illuminating them.

This time, she didn't call out right away, but guided Dayn and Ita to pull the toothcar into a flat area where others had done the same. Carrying their bags, they walked out toward the road's center. Hin met them, and led them back to the Free Winds' building, a broad meeting space with a few closed doors, likely to upstairs rooms by the height of the planked outer walls. Ador was not there yet, nor had any of the leaders arrived. The others who were awake did not bother them as they set their bags down and poured welcome glasses of water from a spout.

Without the bells to guide her, Dime wasn't sure how much of the night had passed. Hin showed them a mechanical device pyrsi here used to keep to the bells without sounding them. To her relief, she saw she had plenty of time before Sol's rise, plenty of time to work. After briefly discussing their plans, Dayn left to find something to eat; there was a kitchen serving hot food just a few buildings down.

Dime was too nervous to eat much—she'd pushed so far with so little sleep as it was and she worried she'd not be able to stay awake after a warm meal. She stood a moment, staring at the wall. Perhaps she could borrow one of the upstairs rooms to start reviewing her papers. Usually even bedrooms held a small table.

"May I ask you something?" Hin's face was drawn.

"Sure," Dime said, distracted. She needed to get the agreement finished and written out before Sol grew close to vis return.

"Is it true that pyrsi might be here from the Circles?"

"Yes," Dime said. "The Light."

His voice faltered. "You'll continue to stand up to them, right?"

"I'll continue to stand up for the pyrsi of Ada-ji. That's what I'm doing." She pointed to the papers.

"You look tired," he said.

She was. She was so tired. So, so tired. "For now, I can't think about it. Is there a place I can work? Without being interrupted?"

"Sure," Hin said, leading her back outside and toward a small tent with a desk, lamp, and a shelf piled with books. A very worn cabinet stood watch on one side, and Dime wondered all it had seen.

"This is where I've been working," he said. "But you can use it."

"Hey. Thanks," Dime said, turning up the lamp and starting to set out her papers.

When Dayn came by with a bowl of split-seed soup, he gazed at her with concern. "If you want more rest, I can wake you up in time."

"I appreciate that. But this is too important." She looked up at her spouse. She wished they could just relax. That their future didn't always depend on another effort. Another worry. He glowed, so beautifully, in the lamplight.

"I love you," he said.

"I love you, too."

She got to work.

Interlude

It was hard enough to move for one, let alone for two. But he had not had enough to drink and now that it was raining, she would not be a good enough neighbor if she did not help him out.

The rain was falling harder now, and she felt sad at herself for being too slow. She grunted and heaved another time, but only fell back into the sand, the rain pelting her face and running down her feathers. If only he would sleep with his face out, he would be with her already, but instead his legs poked out into the rain while his face stayed in the burrow.

He groaned, apologizing. She already knew that he would have to make his way out, to eat and to pee, but sometimes when he'd been sleeping, it took him a while to gather the strength.

The rain was falling now. There was no time to gather strength. The rains moved quickly here and without any dripping or pooling, not like how it'd been in the forest.

She pulled again. Sometimes she pretended he was a very heavy root, and if she just pulled him from the ground, she would have a treasure for the troop. This was very silly to think of a friend as a treasure. But when she did it, sometimes she got thinking about how good a root would be, and then she could pull with more excitement.

With another heave, he slid toward her. And then again. And with a final pull, and now she was getting so tired, he slid out of the burrow.

Glad he was free, she rolled him over until his face was pointing up. His eyes were closed, because the rain would land on them.

Pulling his mouth open, she hoped the biggest raindrops would fall in it. He needed to drink and if she had to be bossy then that was fine, because . . .

She ran down the hill, toward the beach, leaving him in the rain. This was bad, but she did not want him to hear her cries of sadness. You see, when someone got the sickness like this and it was hard to wake them up, there was a time when they did not wake up at all.

Everyone said, no, that doesn't happen, but she remembered that it happened. She didn't pretend a happening like that.

Getting her howls out, she ran back to his burrow. This time, she walked very slowly, like she was enjoying a nice bite of root, and oh there he was.

He was pulling his mouth with humor and that was not something she expected. What, she was funny now? Maybe he could push back into his burrow with that sort of joke.

That was not really something she wanted. She tipped his head back and hoped that he could drink more of the water. If he had enough water, she could bring him some food.

She stared at the rain, begging Sha that it would last a while longer.

Act 2

TO THE CROSSING

Quietly, she scratched the pen against the paper until every last word was complete.

What had she missed? What was left to say? Dime had managed to get the terms of the agreement onto three of the overlarge sheets. First, in draft. Then Volana had arrived, and nervously given her perspective. Over and over again, the fairy had reminded that she'd never worked within the Seats, that there must be aspects she wouldn't know how to address.

"Well, the Seats had epochs to draft their own agreement," Dime had quipped. "And they didn't do it. Nor did they send someone to help me edit. So we'll have to start with this." Feeling that perhaps too far, she tried to say something more helpful. "There are no aspects we all can address. That's why we have to work together." She gazed off at the lamplight flickering against the dark tent wall. That wasn't it either. "Look. You're absolutely right. This shouldn't be one person. It shouldn't be three, or five." She'd been fighting this doubt the whole time. "I have no basis to write this." She swept her hand over the papers. "But they haven't. We can. Right? And if it's not perfect, it's still a start."

That had seemed to strengthen Volana's resolve, and the pyr's help had been invaluable. Even as much as Dime had learned about Fo-ror culture these past turns, there was so much she didn't know, from distinct thought processes to basic terms. Beyond that, Volana understood the way pyrsi reacted and interacted in ways Dime did not. They'd worked together, struggling with how to soothe complex dynamics on a few sheets of paper, until, with the For-or piece refined, Volana left to start organizing the pyrsi who were arriving.

Dime had stepped out for a quick break when Uchitar arrived, just a few takes ago, with Luja and Tum, and Agni with them. Her children looked well, Tum waving from her chair as Luja pushed it forward.

She could see from their expressions it had been a difficult journey along the base of the cliff, but that the worst of Uchitar's tzetz withdrawal seemed to be behind him. Uchitar wavered on his feet, and Luja, providing a brief summary as though reporting in, maintained the premise that he had been the one caretaking for them. There was no question whether Uchitar knew the truth, but it was as though they'd all silently agreed to this version of the story.

Volana must have seen the state that he was in when they'd first returned to Pito and known that he'd used again. She'd seen them talking intensely back at the event space, but Volana said nothing of it now, only hurrying over to greet her friends. She returned quickly to her unrelenting activities: greeting Foundry members and associates as they arrived, and trying to keep everyone calmed and organized as the meeting time approached.

Just as Dime tried to return to her work, Ador and Batu pulled in, together in the back seat of a roomy toothcar. In the front rows sat four enthusiastic assistants who'd taken turns driving at what Ador reported to be a rather fast pace. "Well, we just had the one," Dime muttered, her mind still back in the tent on the sheets of paper.

Dime had not expected Batu's reaction to the Crossing. The fe'pyr was so ready for anything, and yet when she stood out in the gravelly road, her pink suit now draped with a mint green overlayer, and with fairies landing to her sides and conversing with solies, she stood, stunned, with a gaze of pure wonder. Dime would have liked to stay there and help her orient. But she had writing to do.

Volana flapped over again, greeting Batu with warmth and asking if the soly would assist her in arranging the meeting space for the wide variety of visitors. They walked off, Volana saying something about the tent being marked into sections.

"I have a draft," Dime said to Ador. "You'll help me review it?"

With his solemn nod, they walked back to the private tent with its small table and oil-stained lamp. After they'd worked through several of Ador's ideas and concerns, Dayn joined them for a while, reviewing the component regarding the Boring Project over her shoulder. "It looks good," he murmured, uncharacteristically brief, before pushing back through the tent's heavy canvas flap.

With Ador sitting quietly beside her, she began the rewriting process, writing slowly and carefully, and stopping a couple of times to rework a word, which then required a new sheet of paper. "At some point you have to put the pen down," he finally said.

She bit back a sarcastic reply and smiled. He'd been very helpful in catching issues that might cause problems with the Circles, and even had some good input on the Fo-ror piece, in terms of diplomatic nuances Volana may not have considered.

Though she was now fully immersed in her own doubts, there really was just a point where rewriting the piece again would detract more than it would help. So Dime took the three sheets of paper, which right now felt like everything she had ever worked for, and set them carefully between two storage boards Batu had found, held together by a metal clip. Carefully, she slid the boards down into her bag, which would not leave her side until this thing was done.

Hands shaking, she left to a long, plain tent where food and drink had been brought out. She still wasn't ready for a meal, but she knew she should have something. Trying to breathe a little, she walked through the small village, toward where Dayn had pointed her.

As news had spread through the Crossing and even some

outlying villages of the intended meeting, Dime had expected levels of resistance and fear. And she'd seen it: many had immediately fled or closed themselves into their buildings. Yet the Crossing had always been an odd place, and perhaps a longing in it, or to those who knew of it, had been awakened. Dozens of pyrsi were out and lively, as if preparing for a festival biscuit or the arrival of a performance troupe.

Making her way into the tent, she refilled her flask and peeled a warm flatbread from a stack.

"Diamond!" someone shouted. She turned to see a tall soly, wearing the type of clothes typical on the streets and skyways of Lodon. He gestured her over.

"You must be Diamond; you've become so famous lately. Several of us are wondering if we could meet you and hear your story. We're over there." Xe pointed at a large group milling around a table.

"I'd rather not," she said, feeling a sudden lightness, before turning and walking back outside. Maybe, someday, she'd tell her story to more pyrsi, but at a time and place of her choosing, not while she was trying to go about her business and get something done. She ate the flatbread as she walked, glad for its comfort.

"There she is," a familiar voice said, making her heart jump. Dime spun around. Ella made her way over, a light bag slung over her body, and her walking stick deftly tapping against the ground. Rock walked next to her in a protective stance, as if waiting to lend an arm if needed. Rock's tattoos had been drawn on more sparsely than usual, but she'd applied an extra thick layer of blue lipstick, which now turned up in a mischievous tilt.

"Oh, fine," Ella said, a response to nothing Dime had seen. Dime raised her eyebrows.

Rock grinned and lowered her voice. "I can only say this; your friend here is not unacquainted with the history of the Dawn's Circle."

"Hush," Ella said. "Well, look at us. Back here again." It had not really been the eternity that it had felt like since they'd first walked in and paid for a particularly terrible toothcar. Time was a strange and unreliable companion.

"This was Rock's idea," Dime said, pointing at the taller fe'pyr.

"Good," Ella said. "We'll see how it goes, won't we?"

As cheerful as Ella had acted, Dime sensed that she held deep trepidation. This was a relief to Dime. While many of the gatherers were shining excitement and optimism like this was a toothcar party outside some important sports match, Dime felt only worry. What if something went wrong and a War was declared here, because of them? What if nothing happened at all and everyone sped back to their impending destruction? Or even slow deterioration. What other scenarios could she not foresee? How far-reaching were the consequence of their actions?

There was only one thing Dime knew. She couldn't keep living this way. And she would not. If events went poorly here, she'd move back to Lodon. She'd design a lock for her door, if needed. But no more would she be run away from herself, from her beliefs, or from her home.

If it took this ordeal to teach her that, then so be it.

"D." Rock was scanning the buildings. "I dislike being the one to raise a practical question, but are like . . . any of the leaders here?"

"It depends what you mean," Dime answered, knowing full well what she meant. "The Rise is filling now with business leaders, spiritual leaders, community leaders. I mean, you're here." She glanced at Rock. "The Light and High Seat? Not yet."

"Do we need them?"

"I don't know," she said. She really didn't. All she knew is when Sol rose, she was going to present that agreement to whomever was best positioned to sign it. She feared for the reverberations. But she glanced around what were now bustling, city-like crowds. Inaction could no longer stand. Inaction was action now. She feared for her approach, but time was almost out and it was what they had.

A hush fell over the crowd, quickly growing to a roar as everyone looked upward. Then, the crowd quieted again, as the fairies drew near. Though they were only a few pyrsi with nothing to announce them, in the posture, the shape, the formation of the approaching group, there was simply no doubt who this was.

Dime expected more ceremony for the High Seat. She expected fliers, strands of jingling bells, or large banners. Yet the High Seat flew on his own regard, his luxurious robes billowing against the night sky. His three large braids hovered briefly as he landed, then fell back against him.

To one side landed Second Seat Layanie, wearing a rippling, waistless gown of gauzy fabric, then to the other, one of the lower Seats that Dime did not know, in multi-layered robes fixed with a long trail of wooden pins. Three High Guards landed behind them, each considerably older than the other guards she had seen. Dime noted the glint of their diamond pins against the dark fabric. And then finally, Clerk Tikinal. Even from a distance, she felt sure he was looking back at her.

Dime looked around, desperate for an ambassador. She'd been busy writing; she hadn't thought this part through. She ran over to where Volana and Batu were walking toward the road. "Greet them," Dime whispered to Volana. "Please."

"What, but I—"

"Do you want them to be greeted by the mob? Or someone seeking favor?" A group of high-class fairies was making their way toward them with unusual haste.

Volana made a face at Dime, then straightened. With stately poise, she walked over to the group, waving her fingers, as her ribbons trailed her in the breeze.

The crowd quieted as her lilting voice rang out. "Honorous High Seat Ferala, Seat Layanie, Seat Benoio, Esteemed High Guards and High Clerk, we welcome you to this gathering. If you will follow me, I can lead you to your places, then get you anything that you might need."

Dime had a feeling the Seats weren't used to both pomp and hospitality from the same pyr. Then, she remembered that Volana had met two of these Seats, when she'd broken out one of their prisoners in the company of Dime's sassing. She shrunk back a bit. No wonder Volana had given her that face.

Yet the Seats followed Volana off toward the large tent and gave enough of an air of import that no one tried to interrupt them just yet.

Dime let a huge sigh as pyrsi along the path dispersed. Still, she imagined the reactions of pyrsi among the buildings, realizing who'd just passed them. She was glad Volana led straight toward the tent.

While Sol was not yet rising, the sky did not look as dark as it did before. Dime began to worry. Sala said she would be here. Perhaps . . . perhaps Ador could sign for the Circles? Or Dayn? Dayn was in the Circles. But the CC wouldn't be seen as speaking for leadership, not against the High Seat. Or—

A stout soly came running toward them. "Huge procession driving down the hill. We think it's the Light."

Preparing herself, Dime asked the pyr to find Ador, and she walked further down the path, hoping to avoid attracting some of the crowds that had gathered for the Seats. She was glad when Rock ran up to join her. She did not glance around but could hear pyrsi again gathering. Dime tried to breathe calmly as the vehicles pulled down the road, drawing into sight.

Sala did not skimp on ceremony. Her own toothcar held a raised seat, where Sala sat between two large glowing lamps in one of the most fashionable suits Dime had ever seen on her—shades of gold and yellow with layers of tailoring and intricate detail, balanced against sections with no embellishment at all, only showing the quality and cut of the expensive fabric. Heavy fringe surrounded her, tied back in the front, while the drivers below her were nearly invisible over the car's high sides.

Around her were at least a dozen other cars, carrying banners on tall poles. One group sang, as a brass band, seated in a ring of chairs in one of the back sections, accompanied them.

Dime was sorry Volana was missing this. Sort of.

"Here comes the boss," Dime whispered to Rock. Rock was now just . . . gaping.

Ador needed no prompting. He walked ahead of where Dime and Rock stood, with two pyrsi on either side that Dime did not recognize, but who must be pyrsi of high class, by their adornments as well as their demeanor.

"You ok?" Rock asked, poking her a little. "You're sort of falling over."

"Just tired," she said.

"D. Shoot some more brew. This is huge."

Rock's lightness cheered her up a bit, and woke her up too, and she tried to stand properly as Sala was helped down onto the ground and Ador led her away. Dime did not see any members of the Light's Circle. She hoped that wouldn't be an issue.

"I'll, uh, take care of the band," Rock said, walking over to show Sala's entourage where they could rest and find food. "D. Everyone's here. You should get to that tent. I'll be there soon."

Dime took a final break. She used the washroom, washed her hands. Refilled her flask. Then she looked to the pre-dawn sky. The skystones were fading from view and the deep colors were slightly less so.

Her heart seized. While all night she had anticipated this moment, it was drawing forward so quickly now. She stopped, trying to remember all that she had meant to do, when Dayn appeared at her side. "Ready?" he asked.

Dime didn't answer, but walked with him, hand-in-hand, to the large structure and through the flaps of cloth, many of which had been tied open. The interior was packed with pyrsi, rumbling with conversation as well as unease. A wood-planked floor had been constructed over the natural slope of the basin's hillside: a series of wide platforms with several aisles, half made of steps and half built as ramps. A ring of nearly faded glowstones cast the space in an eerie luminance, shining off of the dull, knotted floorboards.

Volana, perhaps Dayn and others as well, had put great effort into organizing the unique space. While some chairs were available, most pyrsi remained standing, grouped onto different floor areas by their affiliation, perhaps. Pyrsi glanced around in curiosity, looking unsure what interactions were permitted. She imagined some didn't spend much time here, but even for those who did, she could see the difference now, of course. At the topmost level, the three Seats stood solemnly, each staring out over the gathering crowd, with Tikinal nearby. The High Guards stood in front of them, on the level below, with rigid stances and formidable expressions that kept anyone curious from approaching.

Next to the Seats stood a medium-sized, round table with a large lamp burning on it. Across the table stood Sala, by herself, and somehow looking at no one. Off to the side, out of the brighter center light, she saw many of her own friends. Ador. Her children. Ella, seated in a chair with her stick leaning against it, not far from Sala. Rock had joined them, leaning against a pole with her arms crossed and gazing at Dime with concern. The rest of the top platform remained empty, with everyone else directed to the other sections.

"Come on," Dayn whispered, and together they walked up one of the aisles. She tried not to scan the platforms, not ready to see pyrsi she might know from the Circles, or anywhere else. She kept her peripheral to a blur of wings and tattooed skin, but couldn't help note when she passed Uchitar and Batu, standing together against the aisle. Batu whispered something, but she didn't quite catch it.

As she approached the front, she saw Ferala was watching her. She looked back at him without reaction, figuring the fear in her own eyes probably said enough. Dime took the last step to the top level and walked to the table, panicking that she didn't have the papers, but then remembering she'd been carrying them in her bag.

"Would you record what happens here?" she asked Ella. Through her nerves, she'd remembered Ella was a journalist. Having a record would be good, if they were going to start this new practice of documenting events for future study.

"It would be my honor," Ella said, pulling a notepad from her bag.

With her legs wobbling, Dime walked behind the table, sat in a chair, and set her bag down next to her. The two leaders still stood to either side, slightly in front of where she sat. Dayn moved just behind Dime, back into the shadow. They no longer touched, but his presence comforted her. She was glad he was here.

It wouldn't be long now. Her heart raced as she pulled the three carefully written sheets of paper from her bag, pressed between the two boards. What would pyrsi think? What could happen? She'd had so many complex thoughts to this point, but the moment nearly here, she was only scared.

Dime didn't know whether the leaders would speak in formal terms, or even make small talk. They did not. Ferala's expression had gone blank, as he and Sala both stared off into the draping sections of roof. Layanie held the countenance of a statue, and only Benoio showed hints of trepidation while glancing around at the crowd. Tikinal had moved off to the side, away. He clutched a notepad against his chest.

As the light grew, Dime wondered, without bells, at what exact moment they would convene. And then, a beam of light burst through one of the open panels, bathing the top levels in bright light. The murmurs dropped to a hush.

Dime rose.

"Hello," she said. While a stride ago, her thoughts had been muddled, seeing the field of shaven heads, styled hair, and quiet flaps of wingtops, her purpose suddenly dawned on her, a weight on her chest. She settled into that weight.

"I am Fe'Diamond of Lodon. If you are here, you likely know some of the disruptions pyrsi have encountered these last turns. What you do not know, as none of us do, is what we have missed all these cycles by remaining, outside of this muted place, apart. While that's been true for all of our lives, certain events have prompted this convergence, and I am grateful we are here together to . . . to try."

She took a breath. "The reason we are here is simply to decide whether a beginning is possible. It is not to answer all questions or heal all wounds. It is to listen. To interact. And hopefully, to leave with signatures on this document." She opened the two boards, jolting as the papers started to slide toward the floor. Next to her, Dayn caught them and helped set them each on the table. He stepped back again.

"This document states that both the Fo-ror and the Ja-lal—ceremonially witnessed by our leaders but with application to each of us as individuals—agree to certain commitments, including continued talks." She turned to face each of the leaders, Ferala first, then the Light. "Please take what time you need to review the document, while I describe it for everyone here." Her hand shaking, she motioned toward the paper. Once she saw the leaders move closer, she turned back to the gathering.

The crowd shifted with tension. Seeing the faces, the discord, she really didn't know how she was able to do this. She couldn't stop now. Like taking a physical step, she remembered what came next: her intro. Despite her nerves, the words flowed from her.

"I could speak more to the background that brought us together, but since we are here, I would like to begin with two things. Things I have learned. Please, I ask you to consider these before you react. First, the idea that listening to another brings the Violence is a lie. Listening, including reading, is the most important thing you can do, for without it, you are trapped within the workings of one mind."

The crowd rumbled. But they craned to hear her next point, and so she waited for them to quiet.

"Second, the idea that offering kindness to another will take something from you is a lie. Lies, as you know, are the Violence, so let us shed these before we begin. And listen together, in peace and kindness. And with the desire to work through our differences without ever again raising a voice or hand in the Violence.

"To do this, we must acknowledge certain clear wrongs. I believe each of you know that there are wrongs, or you would not be here.

This is my spouse, Ma'Dayn, who has worked for cycles in the Construction Circle, an element of the Ja-lal government based in our city of Lodon. He will tell you what he has seen."

Dayn took a step, standing level with his spouse. "The Circles, though I do not believe with the Light's permission, have been operating large drills in the sur of Sol's Reach." He paused. "If you have called it the Barrens, its name is Sol's Reach." A murmur. "These drills, as anyone working in the Seats' complex can attest, put the city of Pito in grave danger, especially given the nature of the Great Cliff and related underground structures, leading into the Heartland. For my fellow solies, if you have called it the Undergrowth, it is the Heartland." He paused for more murmurs.

"I will not speculate as to why someone chose to drill there, but as the drilling took place close to Ada-ji's concentration of diamond crystals and was done, I've confirmed, without authorization from the Light's Circle, I see no reason of peace. No reason of harmony. And so one of the provisions of this agreement is that the Circles cease any geological activity until a joint scientific board—Ja-lal and Fo-ror—can be formed to assess Ada-ji's structure and shape its future."

Both solies and fairies spoke out at this as Dayn stepped back again, each agitated for different reasons. Starting with the Ja-lal had been a risk, but however pyrsi saw her, she was a Ja-lal. And thus she could not justify starting with the Fo-ror.

Dime waited for the chatter to quiet, and she intentionally did not look back at Sala. Not yet. "Please. There is more," she said. "I have seen direct evidence of covert activities originating from within the Seats that intended to put the Ja-lal population in danger from a medical emergency. It is not my belief that this activity was done under direction from the High Seat."

Now she wasn't looking at Ferala.

"And so one of the provisions in this document is a joint medical board, dedicated to oversight of medical facilities and robust communication between them."

There was more to that as well. There was always more. But Dime didn't want to upset the gathered crowd too much, and issues related to the body were sensitive. Seeing that someone had raised a hand, panic from her last public speech gripped her, and she worried that she'd said something wrong, or that no matter what she said, pyrsi would read into it. Another physical step. She took it. "If I could finish, before any questions," she fumbled to say. To her relief, the pyr lowered xyr hand.

"Both governments have wronged each other, as they have wronged their own. There's so much," she stumbled out. "Hemsas. Rations. Bias. Arrest. The blanket acceptance of class in the first place." Hearing pyrsi retort, she raised her voice, determined to get through her statement. "The point is, our governments are imperfect because pyrsi are imperfect. Sometimes pyrsi *want* to cause harm. We cannot deny this. We must work with our leaders, but not trust them without question either." The crowd stirred further. Her chest tightened. "And so another provision of this agreement is a commitment for both governments to reassess their structure."

Among the rising clamor, Hin's elated expression caught her gaze from the front row. It bothered her, and she glanced away.

When she'd wrote this piece bumping along a dark road, it had seemed an obvious need. The faces and shouts of the crowd reminded her what she'd said was basically unspeakable. Ador and Volana had known. They had not stopped her. Well, she couldn't unsay it now. She could only try and calm the reaction. She raised a hand, struggling to keep her voice steady.

"This is not a change. Only a reassessment. No one commits here to any changes to any government structure, other than the promise to meet and discuss, with input from outside the current government structure, and with frequent communication. Some limitations will apply, if our leaders here agree to them, but both governments will operate mostly as they do now until decisions are reached.

"I don't know what a restructure might look like—that's not

something I could draft with one, two, or a handful of pyrsi. But we'll work together. We'll agree to talk. We'll agree to challenge, but not toss out, new ideas. Just like we've all done in our lives in other aspects. But in this case, bigger. With all of us in view. All of us, including those who are not here this turn." As she'd alluded to, there were subterms to the reassessment, mostly temporary limits on specific activities, but she wanted to get the main points out first. "Two more main things. If you will hold the discussions, then I can tell you."

As they settled, she built her courage to offer the final two provisions. She'd known these would be contentious, but she'd considered that having the leaders agree to them now would allow sweeping change for those who needed it now, rather than let the issues linger. She had hesitated to include them, then with the final strokes of her pen, she'd decided to trust her heart. Yet those were the academic arguments of a lone writer. Here, describing the ink on the paper behind her, she doubted what she had done. "Please remember, all of this is in the spirit that working against the Violence, in all its forms, is paramount.

"In that spirit, the next provision involves the influence of the Sol's Pillars within the institutions of Lodon."

Shouts erupted from the back of the space, and at least two dozen fervent, by their tattoos and emblems, Sol Pillars supporters burst forward through the aisles, crowding toward the front of the room. Jaza was not with them.

Rock edged over. "That's Ma'Tanon," she whispered, her gaze fixed on a pyr with an expression that was almost the Violence in itself. "Powerful in their ranks. If he's here and she isn't, he's in charge."

Seeing that Rock had returned to where she'd been standing, Dime turned back. She ignored Tanon. "Hello," she said to the others, sweeping her hand across. "We are here considering a path to prevent the Violence. If that is your goal, please, join us. If not, please remain quiet or leave."

"We will not be overtaken by fairies!"

"Overtaken?" an older fairy shouted. "The Risers have long predicted the brute aggression, and we were right. We must rise; Sha's pyrsi must take their places as leaders of all creatures, great and small."

"Hey!" Dime got the fairy's attention, irritated now as much as scared. "*Rising* is for everyone. If you mean it only for some, then rename yourselves the Sinkers so we can move on."

The scuffle that ensued sounded more like a tavern argument, throwing off the Sol's Pillars, who looked to Tanon for direction. With a quick glance behind, she saw that the leaders still circled around the document, reading it. *Harm.*

Dime almost put up a barrier to protect them. But how could she, not when there was any choice. How could peace ever be reached through barriers. She stood there, trying to think, but disorganized chants of "Sol's Greatness" distracted her. Turning around, she saw Tanon drawing a huge breath, his pointed finger rising.

"Enough!" Rock bellowed from the side, hands on her hips. "If you can't behave, then get out of here," she growled. "Sol. There's a storehouse with kegs that way. If you can't be quiet, at least go have a ferm and stop interrupting us. Go on! Do I have to go serve it for you, like you're petulant ch'pyrsi?"

Rock would give ferm to ch'pyrsi? She couldn't even consider it, as several of the solies and fairies alike did leave, amidst a flurry of shouts lobbed back and forth. Around the room, others grew restless, moving. Speaking to those near them. Arguing, pleading— she wasn't sure in the din. Someone had moved in front of Tanon, and Dime could no longer see him.

Another of the Sol's Pillars stomped toward the table where the leaders now stood, but several others, both solies and fairies from what she could see, stepped in between. After a brief standoff and barked threats, the pyr retreated, shouting caustically as xe left the tent.

She could no longer keep track of the commotion, who was

disrupting, and who was listening. But one momentum overtook the other, and with enough pyrsi telling the disrupters to leave, eventually a tense quiet settled over the space.

And that's when Neimano stumbled in. Disheveled, slow, and with unkempt hair, he marched across the room and pointed at Ferala. "I will tell them what you've done," Dime could hear him say.

The room fell silent.

"Go ahead," Ferala answered, turning first to face him, and then to the crowd. "I will say this first." His voice boomed out. "Let all here witness this and spread my word. Neimano is stripped of all authority and is placed under arrest for crimes against Sha. My word as the High Seat, divined by Sha, binds this."

As the room roared in response, confusion or whatever mix of emotions erupted, and the High Guards stepped forward, Neimano walked backward, glancing from side to side. As he neared an exit, he turned and limped through it. All three High Guards slipped out in pursuit. Dime glanced at Ferala, who looked wholly unnerved, as well as exposed now, the space where his guards had been a prominent clearing.

His head snapped to the side. "Benoio, please," he implored. The Seat—Dime wasn't sure which number—left, following the High Guards, presumably to ensure the news returned quickly to Chambers. Tikinal stared at Ferala from the far edge of the platform, his face frozen. Ferala blocked her view of Layanie.

"We'll handle it," Ferala said to Dime, quietly as the room roared in debate. "But first, I must ask before the others hear. You have included . . . newts in this agreement."

Right. The fifth provision. She had no idea how this would go over.

"Yes," she said. Both Volana and Ador had raised this as a concern, but they'd never been there. They didn't know, the way that she did. She glanced back in the direction Neimano had just left, then back to Ferala. "The Fo-ror will remove the netting. They will also agree to leave Home Sha, the village you call Newt Lake. This area will be a sanctuary for the newts and any the newts allow to reside there. But, yes, pyrsi will have to leave."

"How can I agree to that?" he said, gasping and taking a small step back. Now the gatherers strained to listen, seeing that there was a disagreement at the front. Layanie drew nearer, as if to confer with Ferala.

"A fence and one lake?" Sala stood beside them now. "Do you see what it says about Sol's Reach? That the Free Winds will be consulted on all new projects, while the structural 'reassessment' occurs. Consulted, that means approval. For the Circles! And that hemsa will not be issued, pending a review. How would we protect ourselves from crime? This isn't a reassessment; it's a complete dismantling of our authority. Of order." She swiped her finger up and to the side.

Dime's face warmed. She knew she'd see them as the same, but how could they be open to change if none could be considered? If this was too much, then they should have met the way she'd asked them to, not here, like this. She watched them, hoping for signs of agreement. Each peered down at the paper, regret forming in their expressions.

Dime glanced around. Volana, Rock, Batu, Dayn, and others were walking through the room, talking to pyrsi and trying to keep the commotion down. She saw animated gestures, heated faces, and squints of contempt—pyrsi stepping toward another as if to claim the space. They were losing the calm, losing pyrsi's patience, and Dime herself felt shaken by the vibrations of the Pillars, Neimano's presence, Sala's resistance. All of it. Panic beat in her chest. She spun toward the two leaders.

"Consider what happens if we fail now. Consider it. This room is full of fairies and solies in the same place at the same time for the first time in many of their lives, and—"

"Dime!" Sala cautioned.

"Yes I am," she said, not meaning it to sound the way it did but not wanting to stop. "And if I see any chance that you are willing to let their first exposure together result in the Violence and prove those Sol's Pillars right, I will hold a second ceremony, right now, let the Foundry and Free Winds sign this document, and we will move on without you, with the harmed-off Violence encircling us, if we can't prevent it. This document finalizes almost nothing; it is simply an agreement to begin. The pyrsi here watch you now. Are you here for yourselves, or for Ada-ji?"

Did she mean to say it so harshly? Was that harsh? Maybe she should have slept?

"Don't react," Seat Layanie interrupted. "Look around. Listen."

They stared out at the crowd. Someone had started shouting out Jaza's rally points: fairy invasion, our land, stop them—and others were telling xem to quiet down. From the din, the word "brute" was heard, and then repeated. The language intensified into indistinguishable jumble, like the crackling of fire.

"I apologize for my comment," Sala finally said, to the small group around the table. "The Lake will be difficult. So will many things. High Seat Ferala, I don't know how it is in your home, but in mine the wrong voices have grown the loudest. I am . . . scared. Let Dime finish her statements. Give us another take to think." She glanced over Dime's shoulder, where Ador was now standing.

"I already agree with it," he said softly. "It's a good start. If we got something wrong, we can change it. The terms allow for revision."

The leaders exchanged looks.

"Burgesses," Layanie said, vis voice clear. Everyone quieted, Ja-lal and Fo-ror alike. "Please allow Burgess Diamond to finish her summary."

Dime drew a huge, shaky breath. "The last provision involves return of select habitat to newts." She expected more of an uproar, then realized, likely those most affected were not present. She had not said where, or how much. But with Ferala's commitment, they could begin to work an arrangement. That's what they needed for now.

She looked over to the papers on the table. There were details, but that was it. She'd listed the provisions. All here had witnessed the terms. She felt the energy in the room, the same energy that had brought them here. Tenuous. Dangerous. So, then, how to get them to sign? Sala. She'd asked for time to think. Dime could try. A little longer.

She raised her voice. "Again, the largest issue set forward in this agreement is that both governments will consent to a review, with certain practices limited during that review. No one has set forward what those restructured governments might look like, but we have agreed to discuss it, together. Issues related to ending our separation, as well. The diamond caves. The plains. The forest. Where may pyrsi live and travel?

"Again, this is a start, a commitment to try." While this was true, seeing the intensity of those watching her, it didn't feel like enough. What else could she say? She raised a hand, moving it subconsciously with her words. "We meet here in truth. In truth. It must be understood that the end result may not be the Circles, as they stand, in power. It may not be the traditional structure of the Seats. But the needs of all will be considered and debated, with leadership from the Foundry and Free Winds, working to ensure all voices are heard. With ways to revise when we can improve what we have done.

"We will not be afraid. Policies will be readdressed. Policies on addressing crime, even what constitutes crime. Policies on distribution of resources. On caring for our land. On caring for those who share it. Some will resist these changes, but more will be committed to see them through. Those who resist will only hold the power they are allowed. You are here—I offer you to join the voices of those committed. We must try. For ourselves. For the ch'pyrsi." She raised both arms. "Our goal will be that Ja-lal and Fo-ror will share Ada-ji. In *peace*."

She hadn't meant to conclude, but with the emphasis on that last word, she felt that she had. The room again burst into commentary. Dime heard more shouts among the rumbles. She worried about pyrsi in a tight space with so much change and so many disruptions.

They needed to get the documents signed. Give pyrsi space to breathe. Get outside and allow for questions and discussions. Go from there. Maybe go find those kegs Rock had mentioned. Buy the whole set; Sala surely had the paynotes on her right now.

It was time.

Who would sign first? Harm it, she wasn't going to stand up here and show uncertainty by rolling the dice. Dime was an Intel Agent of the Ja-lal. She turned to Sala, holding out Ferala's gold-embellished pen.

"Would you sign it?" she asked.

Dime's hand wavered and the pen shook almost absurdly. Sala reached for the pen, but as if even holding it would signal her commitment, she held back from grasping it.

Behind her, a body slammed onto the floor. Spinning, she saw that Intinpalo, the Eoch from the Risers was here, and had pushed Hin down. Hin shoved the fairy backward and rolled up onto his knees, and only then did Dime see the sharpened, glinting blade in the soly's hand.

No.

"Dime!" Intinpalo called. The blade launched through the air headed straight toward her. Dime could feel valence now, strong valence, and the blade deflected and clattered onto the floor. Ferala's hands rose and his eyes were wide.

Hin scrambled forward and swept the blade up, but several others had rushed to take it from him. Dime stood, frozen, her arms trembling, trying to think how to help. Everyone moved too quickly; she couldn't see who held the blade, who was in danger. Ferala leapt forward, hands still in the air, his eyes searching for Hin, or the blade, perhaps.

Rock came rolling past Dime like a bowling ball, and wrested Hin to the ground. Dayn leapt toward them both, shouting. Now, Intinpalo was with Rock. The blade flashed and it sliced through Rock's exposed arm, drawing a dark line across her skin. Rock fell backward, grabbing at her bleeding arm with the other, and

Hin swung with his free hand, pushing Intinpalo away, the fairy crumpling over the top step. As Dayn reached the Aoch, a force surrounded them all—Layanie, perhaps—slowing their motions, but Hin slid across the boards and pulled at the fairy's legs, sweeping them under ver as Layanie collapsed with a harsh smack, the sound in sick contrast to the flutter of vis gauzy robes.

In the tiniest sliver of a flash when Dime saw Hin push up, he charged at her, the blade extended. Ferala slammed into him, sending them both to the floor. Dime wanted to help, but it was impossible to see who was where in the tussle, and she did not know how to slow their motion the way Layanie had; she had no idea where the blade was or whom it could hurt.

Ferala shouted something Dime couldn't understand, and he closed in again on Hin, wrapping himself around the younger pyr and pushing them both downward. As Layanie leapt to vis feet behind them, a muffled *pop* sounded from within a sudden burst of blue sparks. The sparks disappeared as both ma'pyrsi—young Hin and elderly Ferala—blew away from each other as if propelled from a force between them. A mix of smells hit her: metal and blood and smoke.

"An explosive," Dayn breathed. "An explosive!"

Pyrsi screamed and pushed and many ran from the tent, its sides shuddering as pyrsi pushed through the overcrowded entrances.

With a howl, Layanie bent over Ferala. Sala knelt down beside him, swearing incessantly under her breath. Sala stood, and raised her arm in full command of the Light of Sol: "No. One. Move."

Before Dime could understand, she saw the blood. Blood, dark and slick, coated the floor, the entire space between the two limp pyrsi. Whose?

Luja ignored Sala's order and ran to the two curled bodies, checking each quickly before placing both vis hands out to warn others away.

"Ve's a medic," Dime forced through her constricted throat. "A medic. Let ver look."

Luja's voice rasped out. "Neither is conscious, as far as I know.

Hin is dead. Harm. *Harm!*" Ve snapped around. "Ma-ma! Hin has two more. Get them away." Ve pointed. "The metal!"

Somewhere from the torn body that had been Hin, two black, soldered clumps rolled out onto the floor. With a burst of valence, Dime swept them up and pushed them, through a wildly flapping entrance and as far up the rocky hillside as she could. As she tried to sense them for a fuse or the like, she found it, and flicking the tiny flints, both devices exploded into the light outside, sending a spray of ash down, like a black rain, to the screams of those watching from outside.

Seeing the blade on the ground, Dime turned her valence in fury, melting it so quickly that the liquid metal ran in between the floorboards, sizzling as it cooled. Her hand, still extended toward it, shook.

"Put valence around me," Rock said. Dime was confused by this next order, but Layanie waved a hand and cast a silvery sheen over Rock, who leaned over Hin's body, prying around, until she signaled back to Layanie, who dropped the shield.

No one moved.

Dime turned slowly, scanning the room. Dozens of pyrsi had pushed back into the tent, some still wearing Sol's Pillars insignia, and some weeping. No one seemed to know what to do. Were they arguing? Should they be?

Could she have done more?

Tikinal, his face drawn in anguish, was seated in the pool of blood at Ferala's side. He stayed silent, holding what remained of the pyr's hand. Luja was speaking to him and to Layanie in a low voice. "He is too damaged. I'm sorry, he won't awake. Anything I could try would insult him further. It won't be long."

Intinpalo was leaned across a chair, moaning, with what seemed to be an injured leg. Rock had taken an offered scarf or sash and was crudely wrapping her arm until it could be properly bandaged. Dime knew Luja carried such supplies, but Rock was not going to interrupt the vigil over Ferala's body.

In the corner, Dayn huddled next to Tum, and he, along with Uchitar, did everything they could to console the ch'pyr's wailing cries as she held Agni tight in her arms. Ella continued to scratch onto her notebook, her face not visible to Dime.

Ador, Volana, Batu—she didn't see them. Were they well? Had they been injured?

Sala still stood, unwavering. Many eyes rested on the Light, waiting to see what she would do. To her back, Tum still cried.

Dime was furious. She was *furious*.

She tried to stand, but she slipped instead, scrambling on hands and knees to find where Ferala's pen had gone. She didn't know whose blood covered her hands: Ferala's, Rock's, or Hin's. She remembered Intinpalo's leg. Perhaps his too. Grasping the pen, she stood, teetering but uncaring, on a chair and held her bloodied hands out for the crowd to see.

"Look at it!" she shouted. "Look at this blood. Is it fairy or soly? Hero? Wicked? Do you even know? Do you want more? Anyone else have a blade, or an explosive? How about our valence! You could knock me over; we could start again. See who dies in the second round. Is this what it took?" Her wits no longer about her, she slammed her hand down onto the signature page, pulling it up to reveal a smeared, ugly stain. "There. There's Ferala's signature. Is that what it took? Is that what you wanted? Is this exciting now? Was this satisfying? Is it worthwhile? Are we serving justice now?"

"D." A voice scratched beside her. Dime looked down, her eyes flashing.

With Rock's gaze leading her, Dime lowered from the chair and held the pen, oddly steady now, out. Sala took the golden pen, smeared with blood, and wrote her own shaky name across the stained paper, pulling out a seal from a beaded pouch which she pressed beside it. She looked across at Layanie, clearly not wanting to disturb the grieving leader.

Layanie pulled a swath of Ferala's robe over his head. Ve stood and turned to face the hushed room. "He is gone." Ve stood straight, wings drawn high, vis chin raised and lip quivering. "I endorse High Seat Ferala's mark." Turning with pronounced clarity, Layanie reached for the pen, then flinched as ve recognized its source. The script *F* seeming to energize ver, ve left a series of marks next to the stain. More of initials than a signature, Dime surmised. Ve set the pen down. Then leaned against the table with both hands, head bowed.

Though the room stilled, Luja, vis mouth twisted, stood and laid a thin blanket over Hin's body. Dime remembered; ve'd had it in the caves.

"Who was that?" someone whispered. A soly.

Dime tried to steady her voice. "Someone who did not want us to work together. But, look, we are working together."

Images of the attack sparked in her mind. She would not honor them here. Searching for a place of calm, ironically, her cycles in government reached out to her now. Process, for all its burdens, could calm. Could regulate. For now, it was what she had.

She addressed the audience. "We have agreed to begin. You must have questions, and we should discuss them. We will talk no more over these bodies. We will talk *without the Violence*. They say this is an open space for meetings, and any can claim its use. As the agreement says, we'll meet here, every ten turns at first light. As it also says, Fe'Volana will lead coordination for the Fo-ror. The Fo-ror government, led by . . . High Seat Ji'Layanie, will coordinate with Burgess Volana on progress and recommendations. If Volana needs time for maternity, Volana will appoint who coordinates for her during that time. That is her choice.

"Ma'Ador will lead coordination for the Ja-lal, working similarly with the Ja-lal government, led by Light Fe'Sala. If there are questions, they will be directed to Volana's and Ador's staffs. Are there any necessary questions? For now?" Her senses were trained protectively on the papers, ready to shield them should anyone approach.

"What about you?" a voice asked.

Dime had thought writing the harmed-off agreement had counted for something. "I'm a burgess of Ada-ji, same as the rest of you. I'll do what I can to help." She sighed, tension escaping like a series of puffs. "We need to treat the bodies." The Ja-lal body would be burned. She forgot whether Ferala's would be burned or taken to Sha, but the Fo-ror would do what they would.

"I'd like to help." A younger fairy Dime did not recognize stepped forward.

"I will not leave him," Tikinal quickly added. "But I would appreciate your assistance." He nodded to the younger pyr.

"I will stay," Batu said, her voice emphatic. Dime turned to see her, eyes red, holding hands with Uchitar.

"I'll help Batu," Luja said.

"I can help with the space," a fairy said. "I . . . help here. I'll replace the floorboards in this section. We'll burn the old ones."

Dime paused. Then nodded. "Everyone else who would like to stay, please, let's go outside, in the light. There's an old tree down the way. Let's meet under it and just get to know each other better. Please. Bring no harm to this gathering."

Dime admitted, she didn't fully know what she was saying at this point. She hadn't slept. She'd been betrayed by one pyr then watched him kill another. Her children had seen. One, now, had volunteered to help burn the bodies. And she knew she couldn't guarantee someone wouldn't bring harm again. Even because of what had happened here. It wouldn't stop them from talking. It couldn't. She was glad to see pyrsi walking, slowly, filing into the light.

Waiting until no one she didn't trust was watching her, she dried the sheets of paper with a slow flow of air and then slid them back between the boards. She handed the bundle to Rock, who slid it into her bag. They'd agreed Rock would guard the agreement for now, and after making a set of triple-checked copies, the original would be hidden until such time there was a central place to archive it. If there ever were.

"D," Rock said. "We need to get word to the newts. To Leader."

"I'll go," Uchitar said. "I can fly, and Tum described the way there."

Rock hesitated. "Uch, we need to make sure they understand there's been movement here. Tell them to hold tight. That's . . . not going to be easy to convey without Tum or Lu."

"They aren't ready to go yet," he said, an edge to his voice.

Dime agreed with that.

"I think I can do enough to stay any action for now," Uchitar continued. "Then we'll get Luja or Tum there soon for more clarity. At least Stern Eyes and Juni know me, and the rest of you are needed here."

"Works for me, then." Rock pointed a finger. "Tell the old one. And I'd have Stern Eyes with you."

"I'll do my best," he said, and Dime and Rock watched as Uchitar made his way outside and took to flight.

"When you're dark, I'll be sure to call you the Old One." Dime attempted a smile.

"Perfect." Rock made a little *click*, then walked outside also.

Luja approached. "I found a fairy medic to set his leg." Dime saw Intinpalo had been situated near the back of the space. "I'm going to help Batu now. You should go outside." Ve placed a hand on Dime's arm. "Go on," ve encouraged, before moving to where Batu knelt.

Dime started to leave, but hearing Intinpalo's groaning, she walked down the steps. The medic was pushing on his leg, fully absorbed.

"Thank you," Dime said to Intinpalo.

He winced again at the medic's prodding. "I'm not sure about everything yet," he admitted.

"You don't have to be," Dime said, going again to leave. Then, she turned back. "But we could use your help."

Not everyone gathered under the tree. Some shaken, disturbed, or needing space, had left. Others kept in smaller groups, their expressions uneasy. Layanie joined those under the tree, wearing plain, borrowed robes, and sat with a mix of classes, in a way Dime suspected ve had not done in a while. Sala sat with some of her entourage, staying off to the side. After a while, Rock returned, wearing a baggy, long-sleeved shirt. Dime suspected she'd used valence to heal the wound, but didn't need everyone to see that just yet. She felt a rush of gratitude. That she'd been here. That she was ok. Seeing her, Rock gave her a tired smile.

Tum left her chair where Dayn had been comforting her, and she walked on her arms toward the center of the gathering. Dime ached at her child's blotchy face, but her heart lifted watching Tum work her way right to the front and center of those seated under the tree. Dayn had slumped to the ground next to Tum's chair, not looking their way. Agni was there, rubbing against him.

Dime stood, awkwardly, as everyone watched her for guidance. Or words. But she was tired. She probably hadn't said everything right. She hadn't worked through, yet, what it meant that she'd brought pyrsi here, given what had happened. What they'd seen. Her eyelids drooped.

"May I speak?" The voice was Ella's.

Dime sat down, grateful, leaning back on her bag. Someone brought Ella a chair, elevating her above the watching rows of co-mingled fairies and solies. She leaned her walking stick against it, then sat tall.

Unlike everyone else, who'd held themselves differently as each event unfolded, Ella looked the way she had when Dime had first met her. A simple tunic. A walking stick. Worn tattoos of fallen leaves over old, dark skin. And sharp, narrow eyes that looked like they could see everything.

"I'd like to tell you one story," Ella said. "And then you can tell me yours. When I was much younger, I met the fe'pyr that would become and remain the love of my life. She was funny. Very stubborn. And immensely beautiful. She was a fairy."

The crowd murmured.

"Yes, a long time ago, by most of your standards. None of this is new. We are only now challenging it. My spouse—" her voice cracked "—would be encouraged to see this scene. But I know what she would tell you. She would say that the rhythm of Sha is an invitation to listen." Ella chuckled, as a few of the fairies whispered to each other. "I think she said it humorously, as it is the lyric to an old song, as many of you know. But she'd probably still say it.

"Pyrsonally, I'd go to Ma'Rorg for quotes."

This caused a stir among the solies. The legendary entertainer's shows, performed almost on the edge of the low city, had been attended fervently by any ch'pyr who could get a parent, or anyone, to take xem. At the time, Dime had thought his message was one of adventure and discovery, and it had been. But only once grown did she realize the profound impact this pyr had had on her and the others who'd been able to attend. Ma'Rorg had taught her that everyone lived in a neighborhood. Not low city or high city. The neighborhoods of community, compassion, and connection.

She wished he were here now. Then, she remembered, he was.

"Love isn't loving a pyr because xe is perfect," Ella quoted. "Love is an active struggle to each reach the part of ourselves that knows we are something *more* than ourselves." She waited a stride, as many of the solies leaned to a fairy to explain who Ma'Rorg was, and others just absorbed the quote.

"We loved my spouse's family. I remember when I met them. Saw my first fairy tree home. Saw how different it was, yet how similar. And, yes, she took me to them, rather well daring them to have a problem with it. They were polite to me on the surface, but could never accept that one of their own could want a relationship with a pyr they saw as lesser. And so she left. While she did visit, mostly in secret, she refused to live in an environment where the fullness of her life could not be accepted.

"I was a successful journalist in the city of Lodon. Lodon was its own case; still is." Several solies chortled, then remembering Sala was literally right there, stopped, shifting in place. "It was strictly against the law there to even associate with a fairy. A secret law, of course. For in a city that never saw a fairy, it could be assumed none had been there.”

While Sala had not been the Light in those days, Dime did glance over at her nervously. Yet, now, the Light sat and listened to Ella, not making any acknowledgment of those who had murmured.

“We moved outside of the city instead. Even there, we were told to leave,” she added. “We didn’t. And I could no longer return to a city that had labeled me a villain, hoping to divert pyrsi from learning my true wickedness. So we lived alone, for the most part. Some, then, could say we had a good life. Living together, each with our true love, immersed in nature and solitude.” Ella adjusted in her chair.

“It was a good life. But it was a difficult life. We were criminals, inherently. We missed our families, our friends. We lamented that the ones who still cared had to greet us in secret. We couldn’t participate openly in careers, in events. We couldn’t be who we were.”

Ella began to grow animated. “Never, ever tell a pyr that the fullness of who they are is not relevant. Never make them hide the nuances of their character for fear of further judgment.” Her mouth clamped shut, and she breathed quietly for a stride.

“There is a forgotten Fo-ror saying,” Ella said. “I came upon it once. It said: ‘Hope is what keeps us going. It is the struggle that takes us through.’ This turn, we were part of the struggle. But in that, I ask you not to lose hope. Those sitting here are undoubtedly rattled by what we saw. Don’t push that away. Talk about it. Talk to each other. Don’t forget what the attacker did, either. Remember a pyr so motivated by lies garnered by another’s self-interest that he would breach our most sacred trust.

“Each of you out there has a choice. You can listen, understand, and hold compassion as your primary virtue. Or you can resist.

“I’ve said too much. We’re all here, let’s all share. Who would like to go next?”

“What was her name?” a soly asked.

“Suzannelina,” Ella answered, her eyes welling. “Suzannelina of the village of Noruh.”

Sometimes straightening up and sometimes leaning forward on her stick, Ella led a stunned crowed through one short tale after another, each pyr revealing something about xyr life, something xe'd wondered, or something that had bothered xem.

Dime could barely continue. Growing dizzy, she walked back, to see Luja and Batu having a conversation. Batu beckoned her over.

"Is this ok?" Luja held a hand forward, wearing one of Ferala's diamond rings. It was huge, and fit over vis thumb. "Tikinal told me to have it."

The token, Dime realized. "Yes," she said. "I trust Tikinal."

"I like him." Luja held vis hand back to vis chest.

Dime turned to Batu. "Are you ok?"

"It's hard," Batu said. Her eyes were no less red than before. "I'd do it the same," she added.

Dime didn't know what to say.

"I won't say his name again, as he died more than once this turn. I won't stop believing in pyrsi. I won't. And I won't stop talking to them. And I won't stop believing that pyrsi can change. *I changed.* And harm if I'm going to let the propaganda be the only voice they hear."

Dime tried to form her thoughts. They were so muddled. "All I can say is this. I could never understand anyone who would say that *you* are the problem, and not . . . that pyr or the pyrsi who taught him what he believed. Knowing it would reach vulnerable ears. The pyrsi who continue to." Dime reached out her arms. "Batu. I'm so sorry."

All three embraced in a hug.

"Ador?" Dime brought herself to ask.

"Time," Batu replied, not meeting Dime's eyes.

The meeting around the tree had grown less formal and became more of a loose gathering. Pyrsi had traveled here for various reasons: curiosity, protest, or support. Now that they were here, together, they talked. Taking on another tone, it now reminded Dime of the late crowd after a festival event: different groups of pyrsi still lingering, finding conversations, finding something special enough not to leave.

Sala had not stopped to talk to Dime before she departed, but to Ador. Ador said there would be more from her soon. "Though she appears calm, I've never seen her so disturbed. She has a lot to consider now. A lot to plan. Ella gave her a preliminary summary of the agreement to take with her, just as Tikinal wrote one for Layanie. She knows she can't pretend this away." His breath in had been shaky.

Even if she hadn't taken Batu's warning, Dime knew Ador wasn't ready to talk about his assistant. When he was ready, he'd tell her. Or tell Dayn. Or Batu. She gave her friend his space as he went to see how Batu was doing. Dime knew her own shock had not yet settled. She also knew that it would, and more pain along with it. For now, she sat back, and just stared out at the sky, peeking over the edges of the rocky basin, with the large tree in view.

A while later, Layanie and Volana walked together, up the hill, having what looked like a very cordial conversation. More than cordial, she noticed, peering at the approaching fairies. They seemed to be connecting. Dime had a sudden sense that they would do great things for the pyrsi of Pito. For the beings of Ada-ji, she corrected.

"Dime," she heard a familiar voice say to her side. She smiled warmly, trying to convey her understanding, as Tikinal landed.

"I'm so sorry for your loss," Dime said.

Tikinal's expression tightened. "I will need to tell his spouse. She has not been so well, even before this." He bowed his head.

"If you need anything, please let me know," Dime offered. She always meant what she said, but particularly so in this case. There was something about the outwardly rigid clerk that had drawn her, even on their first meeting, when he'd saved her from being taken into Neimano's office. She wondered how things would be different now, without that small act.

He and Layanie conversed in low tones, and then left together, as neither the High Guards nor Seat Benoio had returned.

And there should have been no surprise, none at all, when Dime saw a large, bright-feathered figure bounding down the road, carrying Uchitar in her arms like a huge, bouncing, festival doll, heading right toward Dime. Tum must have seen also, because when Dime looked to find her, she was back in her wheelchair, with Dayn helping push her over the rough ground.

"This is someone I must meet," Ador said, walking over to join them, as others gathered and pointed from a distance.

"She might lick you," Dime warned.

"Like?" Ador asked, but then turned, as the newt carrying the grown fairy was an unusual sight.

Juni looked at Dime for approval as she lowered Uchitar down, landing him on his boots.

"That's right," Dime praised, moving to the newt for a not-too-overbearing hug.

"Caught a ride?" Dime asked Uchitar. Then, she remembered, fairies sometimes used fliers. Perhaps they didn't find this as strange. No, it still had to be strange.

"I'm a bit worn out, and she seemed to get that."

Dime smiled, gazing at the young newt.

Juni greeted Tum with great enthusiasm before stopping a bit reverently before Dayn. "Everyone, this is Juni," Dime introduced, but Juni was already deep in conversation with Tum.

"Ok," Tum said, "Juni didn't quite know what Uchitar was saying, but Leader has agreed to wait until Juni gets back. I'm not understanding this next part, but I'm getting the impression there was a little debate about Juni going alone. She kept saying something like maybe Stern Eyes trusts her. She does, or she should. I'm not sure."

Tum spoke some more, her hands moving in the unknown gestures. Juni howled, running over to Dime in excitement.

"Tell her it's not worked out yet! We'll have a lot to do, and I want to get both leaders to meet with them." She rubbed her head, her hair running through her fingers. "I think we can make it happen. There will be snags. But we've at least got them talking about it. And"—this was just as important—"we won't let up."

It took Dime a stride to figure out why Juni suddenly grew more excited, until she saw Ella making her way toward them, her walking stick tapping its way up the hill. Dime turned back, not needing to see whether Ella licked the newt in greeting or not.

As tough as the last turns had been and especially these last bells, Dime was glad to see herself surrounded by her friends, by so many of the pyrsi who had helped her make it here, helped her literally to survive.

Uchitar had found his way to Volana, and they stood opposite each other, holding hands and talking with warmth on both of their tired faces. Their wings fluttered a little behind each of them, as the rest of the world seemed to disappear for the friends. Rock had offered Ella an arm, and Ella seemed to be translating for Rock a whole stream of stories from the white-banded newt as other fairies and solies finally joined them, curious about the large creature interacting so lovingly with the pyrsi. Ador and Batu leaned against each other, their silence providing comfort to each other for now.

Dime stood by herself.

"Ma-ma." She heard the creak of wheels as Tum moved next to her, Agni stretched across her lap.

"Tum Tum," she murmured, grateful to not be alone. Then she saw Luja and Dayn, Luja looking stronger than she'd ever seen ver, and Dayn watching Dime with concern.

"Hey," she said. "I'm glad you're here."

Interlude

Fra's hand paused over the knocker. The privacy turner wasn't flipped, and they'd said they'd be here, but now that she was really at their door, her hand stopped.

Donia ran a comforting hand over her back. He liked touching her back; sometimes she thought it was the strangeness of her not having wings that drew him to it. She didn't mind, though. She liked when he touched it.

"I thought pyrsi lived in towers," he'd said as they walked down the road into her village, only occasionally flapping ahead of her.

"That's in the city," she'd replied. "Towers are too expensive to build outside of it. There's really no need, when everyone isn't jammed together."

He'd winced, maybe thinking it was an insult on city life, which she didn't mean. But pyrsi were accustomed to different things. Donia was from Pito, and he seemed used to pyrsi being jammed together. Fra wasn't.

"It will be much stranger if they open the door and you're standing there like that," he joked.

She wasn't really in the mood for his jokes. The warmth that she'd felt on the way in had suddenly turned to ice.

An image sprung into her mind, of when she'd gone glider jumping. She'd frozen there, too, and then she'd jumped.

Her fingers wrapped around the knocker.

Knock. Knock. Knock.

Fra's heart stopped.

"Pa-pa," she said, as her parther opened the door, wearing a huge, and definitely forced, smile.

Ve swiveled to Donia. "You must be Donia. I've heard so much about you."

Pa-pi was hovering behind ver like a shadow. Pa-pa stepped aside, so they now stood together, Pa-pi's hands wringing. Donia hadn't said anything.

Say something.

"Please, come on in," Pa-pa said. Ve politely told him their names and occupations as Donia walked up the two wide steps.

"No tree shoes," Fra reminded with a whisper.

"What are tree shoes?" Pa-pi asked. "If I may?" Pa-pi always heard everything; she should have known that.

Donia responded too loudly, like he was trying to talk around a marshal. "Oh, we wear shoes for inside, to keep the floor clean. I mean, I'm sure your floors are clean; I just . . ."

"May I see one?"

Donia slipped out one of his tree shoes and showed it to Pa-pi.

"I like this," ve said, handing it back. "Looks comfortable. I wonder if I could get a pair."

"I know someone who makes them," Donia said, his voice a little lower now.

"It's up to you whether you wear them or not. Whatever makes you more comfortable."

Donia slipped the treeshoes back into his side pocket. Fra always marveled how shoes could squish down that flat. But then, that's why they didn't wear them outside.

The group walked in together and gathered around the main living table, to the old sofa where Fra had spent so many years by herself, reading or drawing.

"Can you sit down?" Pa-pa cringed as soon as ve said it. "I'm sorry; please sit down." Ve was totally staring at Donia's wings. "I mean, if you'd like to."

Donia grinned. "We usually sit forward a bit, if we're sitting against a wall. Or one of your chairs, I suppose. Or we can spread our wings, but that wouldn't work much on a shared seat like this one." He grimaced, probably thinking he'd said something wrong.

"I really like your child," he blurted out.

"Donia!" Fra whispered. That wasn't better.

Pa-pa issued a bellowing laugh. "We like her too! So that's one point in your favor."

Fra thought she was going to sink into the floor. She sat on the sofa and tried to get Donia's attention, pointing to the footstool. Taking the cue, he sat down. His wings fluttered conspicuously in the heavily-furnished space.

Once they were all seated, an awkward silence fell over the room. She'd brought a romantic friend home before; that hadn't been so weird. What had they talked about then?

"I saw a field on the outside of the village," Donia tried. "Looked like a sport was being played."

"Yes!" Pa-pa replied, like ve was venting a steam pipe. "We've got one of the best corner-ball leagues in the wes! Do you play?"

"Never heard of corner-ball, but my friends have been trying to talk me into netsack. There's talk now of joining the leagues, cause of all the . . . " Donia didn't seem to know how to reference the meetings and changes going on in the structure of both lands. No one did.

Pa-pa came in with a save, changing the subject back to corner-ball and explaining in more detail than Fra needed, all of its intricacies. She played it, too, but she much preferred playing it, not talking about it.

She noticed Pa-pi's seat was empty. She quietly excused herself to no one listening and walked into the kitchen.

"Are you ok?" she asked, the words grating out. What if ve said no?

"I'm not sure what to say," ve answered. "He seems very normal."

That was a separate discussion, but she knew what ve meant. "Pa-pi, he is normal. I'm the one off-kilter."

Ve laughed. "I can see that you like him," ve started to say, then caught Fra's eyes.

What?

"Sorry, I don't mean to be so pyrsonal. You more than like him. I'm sorry. I just could . . . see it."

She did. Fra wanted to spend every day for the rest of her life with this big, beautiful, clumsy, fairy, and all she wanted was for her parents to be glad.

Looking over at what Pa-pi was doing, she saw ve had unwrapped one of the good cakes. Ve never unwrapped the good cakes.

With a nervous smile, ve picked up the carved silver tray, and carried the cake through the doorway.

Fra hurried to join ver.

Act 3

COVALENCE

Dime poured a cup of brew. Since moving into Ella's Tower—she just couldn't stop calling it that—she hadn't had a bad cup yet. Hopefully Ella would keep bringing by new bags.

Not wanting to leave the regiment of bells behind, and besides, it came in handy for running a school, she and Tikinal had compromised on a rather docile chime. Connected to a rotating device like those at the Crossing, this one would chime along with the bells of Lodon, loudly enough to be heard in the tower and its grounds but not in the nearby tree home where Tikinal and Anathatu lived.

As the spindly old woods trees weren't as massive as the spreading trunks of the Heartland, their home had required extra construction to keep it secure. The resulting effect was that the rooms were each on a slightly different level, like the home was walking up the trees.

A ramp had been built in for those who couldn't fly. While this had been planned from the beginning, it also helped with the wandering home issue. The ramp, built to swirl up the base of the included trees and then through the home itself, added great charm to the composition, she thought.

Tikinal had been particularly specific about making sure Anathatu had a separate room for his writing. "He's never had a proper room," Tikinal said. "Our home in Pito was nothing to complain about, but the room he wrote in did border a park that was constantly filled with ch'pyrsi. Ch'pyrsi may be Sha's gift, but they are *not* so conducive to writing." And, so, Anathatu now had a carefully designed space, higher in the trees than the rest of the home, dedicated only to his writing endeavors.

Ella's tower had only been given a few changes. A bucketpull had been added to the back of the tower staircase. It was a simple one, designed to reach the main, second floor. Dayn had worked with some contacts within the CC to get it finished with old stones that blended in with the rest of the weathered tower. They'd been so excited to tour the unique home, they'd been eager to assist. Other than that, the small tower had benefitted mainly from a few minor repairs, as well as the addition of a more formal outside patio, decorated with comfortable chairs and colorful, shiny orbs resting on wrought metal stands.

Two more buildings completed their little campus—first, the primary classroom, bunk, and side practice areas, and then a separate workshop and living space for Tum. Using their toothcar, which also facilitated occasional trips to Lodon, Dayn took Tum to classes in a wesside village, to make sure her basic coursework was completed. But mostly Tum focused on her small-object carpentry, which was growing quite advanced, Dime thought with pride.

Tum really seemed to love living here. They all did. Now that the Circles had admitted, with an apology, even, that the wesside strip of land was not actually haunted or hexed or whatever, building in the old woods was formally restricted while longer-term plans were being figured out. Ella's Tower had been granted special status, on account of both Ella's history as well as the nature of the school now being run there.

Ella had been arguing for the whole area, up and down the rocky coast, to be dedicated to public use: some sections left unoc-cupied by pyrsi, some undeveloped land used for the study of life, as well as some grants for artistic schools and retreats. She'd also been encouraging pyrsi to plant trees where they lived, to try and revitalize the plains to what she insisted they used to be.

Dime sat at the table, taking another sip of the steaming brew. The mail carrier had brought notes from some of her students, but she'd waited until she had some quiet to read them. One of the return marks jumped out at her. This was not a student. The markings were from a medical enclave, but it wasn't Luja's handwriting. Besides, Luja never wrote; ve only stopped in. Usually unannounced.

She opened the note.

> *Dime,*
>
> *I hope you don't mind me reaching out. (It seemed fair, and I say that with lighthearted intent.) Word reached me of the work your child was doing into researching blocked interferers and whether they could be reliably purged from a pyr's blood. It is touchy and careful work, and I suspect perhaps more than a single pyr can achieve in one lifetime.*
>
> *I wanted you to know I've reached out to ver to ask if I could assist. I've even offered to donate samples of my own blood, though it will be a while before ve can design a reliable test to even use them.*
>
> *You must be very proud. Ve is entirely charming and earnest.*
>
> *My best to you and your family,*
>
> *Olok*

Charming and earnest. Well. She must also think ve was talented, if she was willing to work so closely with ver. Dime stared at the paper a long while.

Telling the other survivors about the disease had felt necessary. At least, the ones she could. Jaza had not been seen in Lodon since the Meeting. More than not seen, Enforcement had found that all the core meeting places of Sol's Pillars had been burned to the ground. There were no injuries; they'd been empty, but Jaza's parting act of the Violence had been a dramatic statement one way or the other.

Everyone kept asking Dime why. She had her theories, but they touched onto pain the others couldn't understand. She deflected the questions; she changed the subject. Dime saw no defense for Jaza's harm, nor did she want to discuss her departure. Rumors had popped up here and there of where pyrsi believed her to be, but as long as she didn't interfere in their efforts, Dime had better things to worry about.

Nafat had taken the news in stride; he'd been more interested in telling her all about his efforts working with the Fo-ror. Per her wishes, Dime had not stopped in to see Olok directly, but she'd delivered a sealed note with just enough vagueness to protect Olok if it was seen by someone else. In that, she'd asked Olok to inform Kolk, in whatever way Olok thought appropriate.

Dime still had not found Cren, nor even had proof if the pyr was one of them. The traveling vendors guild had offered to deliver a note to each village they visited, simply saying if Cren saw the note and wanted to talk about things they had learned, where Dime could be found, here, at the tower.

As for the deceased, Dime left them alone. Left their memory and their families to the life they'd had.

A flurry of frantic footsteps pattered up the staircase. Dime turned around. "Agni, what is it?" Something had the kita excited. She began to turn in circles and mew. Tum and Dayn couldn't be back yet; they'd only left for the village a bell or so ago. Maybe Tikinal and Anathatu? They'd been gone a while.

Then she recognized the voice at the door. She hurried down the stairs.

"Ella!" she said, joyful to greet her friend.

"Am I interrupting?"

"No, not at all." They walked up together. "It's just me, Agni, and Friend. We just finished a class set. No students here for the next two turns, so I'm able to plan a new set of lessons. And maybe clean up a bit." She glanced around the room nervously, noting it was much less meticulous than Ella had kept it. "Tikinal and Anathatu flew into Lodon for a while. Dayn is out with Tum."

"I like it that way," she said, barely lifting a finger to point toward Dime's hair.

Dime actually hadn't planned for it to be seen this way. She'd kept growing it on the top, but not used to the distraction, decided to trim the sides. Often she let the longer section curl, but since she'd thought she'd be here alone, she'd braided it back over the top of her head, mostly to keep it out of her face. She decided not to read into Ella's praise. "Thanks!" she said, reaching up to pat the braid. "Would you like some brew?"

"No thanks," she said. Ella looked uneasy, a trait in the Dorh Dime wasn't used to seeing. Ella would tell her, whatever it was. She waited.

"I think I've found the right place for Friend."

Ella had not wanted to cart the old, needled plant into Lodon, where she'd been staying. Yet, Dime had always suspected she wouldn't leave her companion here indefinitely. They'd been through too much together. And if Ella was willing to move it, then wherever they were going was likely intended to be permanent.

"I'm moving to Pito."

Wow. Dime tried to think what to say. All she could come up with was, as usual, awkward. "Oh, that's great. Change of scenery, or do you have specific plans?" It was a vague enough question so as not to pressure Ella into answering, she hoped.

"Volana would like my help."

Now that really was great. Dime began to think of all the ways Ella might help the governance talks, with all her insight and wisdom.

"They've agreed to give her a larger space, with one of my own adjacent. I talked them into a set of proper stairs, and pulled a favor with a friend I trust to build them." She patted her leg. "Ramps do poorly for my knees. If I need mobility later, maybe I'll cave and use those fliers." Dime was on a pyrsonal mission *not* to travel by flier, but saw no reason to say it.

Then, Ella was going to live in a tree. For a stride, Dime figured they would have built her something on the ground. But why? If Ella wanted to be in a tree, she should be in a tree.

"How's the ba'pyr?" Dime asked. She wanted to get to the Heartland to visit Volana and little Sashaille, but running the music school had proven a much more time-consuming endeavor than she'd anticipated.

"Doing so well. Showing signs of flight already! And what a pair they make." Ella paused. "Eytanii showed up again, suggesting they should work things out. She held firm, but I know that was difficult and she doubted herself as well. Her mothers have been keeping her distracted. I think he's got the message now. Oh! And you won't believe who helps her. Sometimes even watches the ba'pyr, not that I can endorse it. That old grumbler, Intinpalo."

"Intinpalo? Helping with the ba'pyr? Or the meetings?"

"The meetings, sorry," Ella clarified. She leaned against her walking stick. "He's a bit of an ass, but he knows a lot of pyrsi and knows how to speak their language. It's going very well. He's sped progress a great deal."

"I admit, I haven't kept up with the latest on the talks." Dime hadn't. The school took all of her time and then some. She wasn't complaining! It was just a ton of work. Luckily, the Circles had made sure she had whatever resources she needed, knowing the value of their work here.

"It's rocky," Ella said with a shrug. "Don't think anyone thought otherwise. Pyrsi are so used to nine Seats, they act like it's the only construct that could exist. Harm, sometimes we talk about the newts just to distract pyrsi from themselves." Dime knew pyrsi had been particularly hostile toward the provision regarding the newts, and that Ella had been relieved when they'd finally broken through. "Have only cleared one corner of Home Sha, but at least it's getting some of them back there."

Dime had a feeling it might clear out more quickly once the newts were back. She also noted that Ella had centered her updates on the Heartland, as if her focus were already there.

"That said, I think the Seats themselves have accepted they can't remain in their current form," she continued. "That's probably the biggest step."

"What about the prisons?"

"Those arrested for drug use have been released. Some expected the debate to draw out, but the only pyrsi with any real knowledge of tzetz at the hearings were those advocating for the prisoners, so the change blew through before many realized what had even happened. As part of the agreement, Volana set up recovery, counseling, and community centers around Pito, for those affected to gather and seek support.

"Others are being reviewed case-by-case. A few pyrsi released, but most still suffer. The main hold-up is the discussion on pyrsi who may pose a risk of the Violence to others. They are struggling to talk about it, of course, as they've spent so long pretending there was no such thing amongst their own. But one of the main reasons they started putting pyrsi out of sight was it was easier. For them, I mean. Now that they need to develop solutions, they're spinning.

"This is all complicated by the fact that Neimano is there. What do you do with a pyr like that, who shows no signs of developing empathy, no ability to correct his behavior? Once the truth of his actions, really only the edges of it, began to seep out, pyrsi were understandably disgusted. They aren't eager to send him back out on his way."

Dime felt the same. She didn't like the idea of anyone in captivity, nor could she reconcile the risk he posed to others. From what she'd heard, Ulkanet had been found and arrested as well, pleading that everything the former High Guard had ever done was at Neimano's orders. She was sure that was true, though she didn't think that made an excuse. Neimano's other High Guards had all been dismissed—and offered roles outside of the government.

"So what do you do with him?" Dime asked. It seemed naïve to think only one pyr like Neimano could ever exist.

"There's talk of some sort of marker. To warn pyrsi. To restrict where he can linger."

Oh, Dime didn't like that. That sounded like hemsa all over again. Ella read her thoughts. "It's not the same. It's not digging up every thing a pyr ever did and throwing it back at them forever. It's marking pyrsi who actively pose danger now, and removing it when it's determined they do not."

"I don't know," Dime said.

"That's why we're still talking. And he might not be capable of following that guidance either; they may need to accept that some few pyrsi simply must be contained. But we'll get there. Just because the answers aren't easy doesn't mean you stick with the ones you know are bad."

"Ma'Rorg?" Dime asked.

"Nope, that one was me." Ella smiled. "And wait until they start thinking about the diamond caves as well as exploring the structure around them. That, they're still putting off. Mind if I get some water?"

"No, sorry, of course." Dime was such a terrible host. She did try. Giving up on fixing it herself, she instead sat back as Ella rummaged through the kitchen, murmuring under her breath. Probably that Dime had put things in the wrong spots.

Ella returned to the table with a tall glass of water. She seemed to have also found a curl of preserved teal rind to loop over it. One of the good ones that Rock had brought her. "I stopped in to see Luja," Ella said, nibbling at the end of the rind before pushing it down into the water. "Your father takes no issue with the extra attention."

Dime chuckled. That was indeed true. Though she missed having Luja around turn-to-turn, the arrangement helped everyone out. Gorg didn't live so far from where Luja was working. He'd been having some issues with fatigue, and having Luja around to take care of more physical tasks eased his load. She'd worried, somewhat, that Luja was too independent to live with vis grandfather, but it didn't seem to bother ver at all. At least now, while ve was so focused on vis research and also on volunteering time to Ador and Batu's efforts.

The Free Winds had changed in nature, as the culture of discussion had spread now, outside the walls that Ador had secured for it. Pyrsi like Luja actively pushed this change: hosting meetings around the city to gather feedback on the ongoing plans and pass it back to the larger group. To get pyrsi used to gathering, used to talking, not scared to offer new suggestions, even if others disagreed with them. But since the Free Winds were the point organization for funneling public feedback into the reassessment process, Ador kept the name and structure for now, though he often suggested it would also change along with whatever government the reassessment proposed.

As for the Sol's Pillars, Tanon still tried to keep them going, stronger than ever as he said, after the governments had betrayed them. Again, his words. He frequently spread the 'simple fact' that a Free Winds' participant had brought the Violence to Ada-ji, and yet the Free Winds were now shaping pyrsi's lives. While this was true without context—*only* without context, making it *not* true in Dime's view but Dime was not everyone—it infuriated her that he could taunt Ador, who had suffered enough, this way. That he could obscure the fact that the pyr's act had been incited by his unnuanced anti-government sentiment and fear of change that was entirely the Pillars' message, so different than the thoughtful challenge of power that Ador had promoted.

Tanon pushed on, morphing his messages to each audience with more skill than Jaza ever had, and Dime worried how much he'd be able to undermine their efforts. Finding their banners and meeting locations all burned, and presumably by Jaza herself, had been a morale dent for sure, as had her disappearance.

But that wasn't the biggest challenge that Tanon faced.

First, there was simply the fact that solies and fairies of all classes were meeting and talking. And pyrsi found that they liked it. Often the cultural differences caused discomfort—or even charges of offense—but more often they caused exploration and then joy. Discussions of wrongs could never be easy, but there was so much power in them, pyrsi were now clamoring to have those talks, wanting to understand, so that they could move forward. And eventually heal.

Through all those interactions, wearing Pillars insignia had started to become . . . uncool. They had represented themselves as upholding the ideal of protecting what one rightfully had, but with open dialogue, pyrsi were seeing for themselves that the Pillars promoted inequality and division. It was harder to latch on to an idea that was fundamentally unkind when pyrsi discussed it as such. Pyrsi who stuck to wearing their symbols were offered a tight grimace or passed by quickly. With this, some of the more casual followers had quietly dropped out, at least from open participation. The more vocal ones were still an issue.

She was certain they had not heard the last of the Pillars, but with sustained effort, their influence would continue to lessen.

To each of Ador's meetings, he brought different speakers. Pyrsi affected by hemsa or limited by their class, to explain their experiences. With Ella's prompting, pyrsi began to document their speeches, print them, and make them available throughout the land, not just in Lodon. Dime hoped this was helping. Ador had also seen the need to get groups traveling outside of the city. He'd committed to working it.

Frankly, Ador needed purpose to push him forward these turns. His assistant's betrayal had shaken him more than it had most of them, certainly more than those discussing it from the outside. Most pyrsi simply thought he felt responsible, but Dime knew it ran deeper than that. Ador had gotten to know the pyr, knew the struggle of his upbringing. Knew that he had good characteristics to him. It was much easier for pyrsi to condemn someone they'd never met. Ador deeply condemned what he had done, but he'd lost someone he'd known and cared about. He'd lost a piece of his own trust. Dime felt for her friend.

She also knew that blaming specific pyrsi was easier than examining society at large. Zealots against change revealed themselves in time, but they grew from the vines of the soft prejudices and gentle protection of inequity, the very philosophies Ador had worked to root out.

It helped Dime that she'd been there. Helped her to understand. Everyone who'd been there that day was changed, and shared an understanding that others simply did not, even when they thought they did. It was different to discuss the idea of War than it was to see it employed. To see someone kill another to further xyr own goals, to see the bodies lying limp and destroyed. Dime shoved the image aside.

They wouldn't forget that. They wouldn't forget why it mattered.

Dime thought about Ella moving to Pito to help Volana with their reassessment efforts as well as Foundry coordination. She and Volana would make a powerful team, old and young working together with the combination of their insight. Dime, whose gaze had drifted to the window, looked back at Ella. "You're moving to Pito, then. You must be excited."

Ella nodded. "I truly am. I'll miss the old woods, but I've had plenty of time here." Ella certainly knew she could visit anytime. Dime had also told her that a hundred times now. "A part of me has always regretted Suzanne not getting to go back, and perhaps in my own way, I'm taking her home now. Though, she wouldn't imagine me working with the High Seat."

Dime wasn't sure about that.

"We're still calling ver that for now. It eases the transition for those with trepidation. But ve agrees it shouldn't stand. In fact, ve's already changed vis demeanor so much. Look, you'll never shake the sprinkles off of a cake like that, but for how many years ve was entrenched, I'm delighted by how quickly ve's adapting. Ve and Volana have become very close, which is a better illustration of how the whole structure was bunk in the first place than I could provide."

She sat down the glass. "Do you know what I think?"

"What?"

"I think they'll put Volana in charge of the whole thing or at least one of the prongs if they go a more division-of-roles way, and I think Layanie will end up on her staff or whatever they'll end up calling it. I know. But I think that."

Dime had given up on thinking things couldn't happen a long time ago. Speaking of which. "What about more of a joint structure? Is that still being discussed?" Ella would know she meant between Ja-lal and Fo-ror. No one thought pyrsi were ready for a single government, and Dime herself wasn't convinced there should be one, but she hoped for closer ties, as so many issues affected all of Ada-ji.

"It is. At least for now, I see it more like both cultures coordinating than any sort of merger. That may be where we're at. May even be where they stay. Honestly, that will be the easiest part. The biggest hurdle they face now is what to do about rations. Not just food was rationed, you know, but housing. Labor. If a pyr had servants, it's because the Seats said they should. As some pyrsi received such a disproportionally high level of resources *and* thought they deserved it, there is simply no way to rework the system without some of those pyrsi receiving less. For some, a lot less. Once the high-class see those proposals, many of their smooth and benevolent cooperation will quickly bristle."

"How do you think they'll do it? The government, I mean."

"I think they'll have to rework the whole structure, and I think pyrsi are going to have to speak firmly that this is simply the way things need to go. It might have to be done in steps, and it'll have to follow a huge cultural shift. Pyrsi repeating and refining their tenets until the pyrsi who don't follow them fall by the wayside. Recognizing that there's more pyrsi who want balance than there are who don't. Until some pyrsi are simply told they are out of line with society's well-being. If some pyrsi are going to have more than others, the rest of society has to think there's a justification for that. At some point 'because they had it before' won't be enough." She looked up poignantly at Dime. "That's why what you've done resounds so deeply."

"What do you mean, the Agreement? Many of us worked on that."

"You really don't see it, do you? You didn't just take a step; you took a leap. No one expected that. All you had to do was convince them to start agreeing to meetings, and to address the immediate issues of Neimano and whoever was directing the boring.

"Instead, you made the pyrsi see them—really see them—and you made each government agree in front of a wide range of burgesses that a full reassessment was needed, even if it wasn't practical to address it all at once. That it wasn't just our lack of talking that kept us apart. It was direct control by those in power. Power that was given, not presumed. And then when the attack was barely complete, you challenged each leader in front of an audience to be the first to stand up and say, no, we won't promote peace here in the literal reflection of blood because we have to maintain our control. When you challenged them to *say* it, it was simply indefensible. The most trouble we get into is when we let them not say it."

"Oh." Now Dime wondered, if she had understood how far she was reaching, would she have done it. She was just . . . upset. And tired, too. It had seemed right.

"And then on top of that, Pillars and newts!" Ella stopped a stride, coughing into a tissue. "There is no question what we've done is only a beginning, and undoubtedly set to fail in many ways. I can't imagine the cycles it'll take to get this right, and since I don't have so many left, I'm not sure I want to. But pyrsi are working now, they're talking, they're challenging. Pyrsi like Volana are allowed their voice, and pyrsi like Layanie can help advise it. It's progress."

Ella was sure making progress sound stressful.

"Hey. I'll cheer you up," she said. "I saw Uchitar last time I was down there. Ok, I intentionally stopped in, which he knew. He asked, 'Here to check up on me?' and I responded, 'Of course I am; what did you think would happen?' Anyway, he's doing great. Part of the solution is just being surrounded by pyrsi who care, pyrsi who keep him talking, who care enough to distract him when needed. He has a new brightness to his eyes, a presence that inspires his team. He seems almost happy."

That did cheer her up. Uchitar had helped with the construction of the school, but then Nafat had brought him in to help build a soly cultural center in Pito. Dime hadn't been sure the Fo-ror would grant the land use or the assistance, but Nafat could be rather dynamic when he wanted to be.

"It was rocky for a bit," she said, referring still to Uchitar. "Some of the area residents learned that one of the pyrsi doing the work was 'from the canals' as the more polite ones would say—and they stopped by the construction site to express their concerns. Pyrsi often disappoint, but sometimes they triumph. From what I heard, the pyrsi Layanie had put in charge, who'd been working with Uchitar, told the visitors exactly what they thought of that and encouraged them to be on their way."

"That's great. Honestly, though, I'm trying to imagine him working with Nafat."

Ella laughed heartily. "It's true! They clash constantly. But the artistic result of it is great. Nafat knows soly architecture—his understanding of detail helps the project tremendously—but he's never built it. Uchitar has such a good sense of how to effectively make something both beautiful and practical. When he visited Lodon, he learned a lot about the style and techniques, and as you know, Dayn got him a crew of those familiar with tower building and repair. So together they are creating something really special."

That was true, about Uchitar's interest when he'd been in the city. Dayn had taken the fairy to meet with willing CC members, and apparently they'd talked so long Dayn had even fallen asleep in a chair at one point.

While Dime was glad life was improving for her friend, she still worried for him. If Uchitar had connected with his family, Ella would have mentioned it. Dime didn't know if that was a skybridge collapsed by this point. She knew that lingering sadness would make it difficult for Uchitar to fully move forward. "It's still got to be hard," she said.

"I know," Ella agreed. "But he's working, making friends, and keeping busy, and for now I will celebrate those victories. If his children would see him again, it's going to take time. You can't fully blame them for that, could you?"

Dime wasn't going to blame anyone. She hadn't lived through either experience. She just knew how much that ba'pyr had meant to Uchitar, and she hoped they'd find a way to connect.

"Speaking of construction, Dayn had some good news as well," Dime said. "Regarding the geological board— Sala is working with him directly, and since he's no longer in the Circles, he's making good progress outside anyone's windowview. Though of course the board itself will document discussions and make those available, once it formally starts.

"Sala has taken a less active role in the meetings over the government restructure than Layanie has. She's really deferring to Ador, almost like she's no longer seeing herself as part of the restructure, before that's even been settled. Most of her work has been behind the scenes. It's taken a great deal to keep the members of the Light's Circle from throwing out the Agreement and taking over themselves. In fact, that's the only reason she hasn't just stepped down. I really think that."

Ella nodded. "They wound themselves into that knot. By making the Light's power unquestionable, they can't just toss her out then presume to have that same authority themselves."

"Right," Dime said. "And knowing Tanon's group is looking for a reason to show they've failed lingers on their minds as well. So for now, Sala is keeping them either engaged or away, depending on the pyr, until Ador makes enough progress. Their hope is, once they start moving influential pyrsi into these new processes, by the time they start to argue they'll see that it's already been set up, past their naysaying. I mean, it's all out in the open. But you know.

"Meanwhile, Dayn and Sala have been trying to get to the bottom of who modified the Boring Project and how xe kept it secret. It's been an IC-worthy covert operation. They've tried to act like that question has slid by, when it hasn't. They are keeping the investigation as quiet as possible, but Dayn has indicated they are close. We will make sure whoever put everyone at such risk is found and xyr reasons understood. They haven't decided what to do with xem, but xe'll be kept from positions of power. And with hemsa suspended for now, well, like you said, it's challenging but they'll have to figure it out.

"Beyond that, the boring caused a great deal of damage, all the way from the eas side"—she still wasn't going to say the Underground out loud—"to the Crossing. Dayn is working to get more resources allocated to deep research and rebuilding. Maybe even some modification of the cliff structure itself, which would also make it easier for travel. He says there are implications to how the Great Cliff impacts animal habitats and water flow. Like it didn't use to be there." Dime stopped, seeing Ella lean her head lightly against her hands.

Ella sighed, rubbing her temples. "I'm sorry. When I start to think about all the challenges, I get tired. And that's why what you're doing is so important."

What I'm doing? For a stride, Dime wondered if she was being sarcastic. But Ella wouldn't be, not about this.

"Yes, this." She briefly extended her hand. "It's important. Art heals. It connects. It teaches. It calms. It reinvigorates." Ella scanned the tower room, the one where she'd spent so many cycles. "I couldn't imagine a better use for this space. I'm glad we stayed here."

Dime presumed Ella was referring to a choice Ella and Suzannelina had made, to live here rather than live a life together in the Underground, a place where they could have been together, around others, in a life that even seemed normal at times.

Ador had returned to the Underground and told them about the Meeting, as it was now called. He'd seemed a little disappointed in the reaction, enough so that he hadn't gone on too long about it. From what Dime had gathered, many of the pyrsi there had been glad to hear of the progress, but mostly asked for more time.

Bown had specifically pulled him aside and pleaded for continued secrecy. Ador had sensed not just fear for themselves, but also a concern about whether others would try and move in and change the culture of a place they'd cultivated for so long. For now, he was letting them be but it was just another complication, another angle to address.

Some at the Underground had left, after swearing they would not reveal where they'd been, some of them for cycles. Dime could only imagine the emotions involved in those returning to their own homes, or wondering, now, what place they could call home.

A bird was singing outside the window where Friend rested, and Ella stood to go watch xem. She was murmuring to the plant, running her wrinkled, dark fingers through its needles. Dime could see the plant had perked up. Yes, it would be much happier being back with Ella. Hopefully she could make her arrangements quickly, and the plant could settle back in.

"I'm planning to go see Home Sha myself," Ella said, still looking out the window. "Maybe see if I can convince some of the holdouts why we are all better with the newts and other beings having a place to thrive, before we have to get more direct with them. And I can reassure the newts we are working it."

Dime would enjoy that. "Maybe I can go with you?"

"I'm in the middle of arranging my move. I planned to go a few turns from now."

Classes will have restarted by then. If she was going to go, it was better to do it now. She looked over at the stack of papers. She had to get those lesson plans done.

"Just go," Ella said. "You don't need me there. Take Tum. She'd love that."

"She would," Dime agreed. "But next time, I'd love to go together."

"That's a deal," Ella said.

Though Tum preferred to travel on the ground, she did agree that as far away as Home Sha was, it would be better to fly there than not have time to go at all. With tools and resources to make the platform properly this time, Dime pushed Tum up onto the wooden rectangle. She sat down in her own chair, this one bolted down.

"Wheels locked in?"

Tum nodded enthusiastically. Dime had not had time yet to go looking for her original flying chair for sentimental purposes or perhaps a nice garden sculpture, but one of these turns she would. As for Volana's dining chair, a family of barips had made their hut into a home and so Dime had left the chair there, for whatever purpose they'd claimed it. Pyrilee's chair had replaced it at Volana's home, and of course Rosebench was now the centerpiece of Rock's living space in Lodon.

She lifted them up into the sky.

Tum, in her excitement, managed to chatter almost the whole way there.

It was nice not having to hide. Not to say that all fairies were comfortable with the sight of her flying platform or wingless beings in general, but the laws were changing. Minds were changing, all around. For the rest—frankly, they could get over it.

Home Sha was easy to spot. Other than Sha verself, it was by far the largest body of water she'd ever seen, blue brilliance sweeping out like welcoming arms. While its beauty would not be concealed, the toll of the last cycle or so was apparent. Hasty structures speckled the trees, and one large clearing was covered with ground-level homes, similar in layout, but not design, to the ones dotting the plains of Sol's Reach.

The trees were thinner than they should have been. Though fairies were generally good about leaving the structure of the forest, here pyrsi had clamored to create more views of the water, leaving large gaps in the branches that Dime knew would take many cycles to even start to regrow. She imagined the pain this must have caused the newts when they had first seen it, knowing their acute connection to the land, and especially this land.

The wedge that had been cleared for the newts' return was smaller than Dime had envisioned. The homes had not been torn down, so the structures stayed in the trees, and Dime could see newts hanging from their beams or sitting on the roofs, grooming or enjoying the warmth of Sol's light.

Newts crowded the shore. While most stayed to the assigned corner, others were pushing the invisible boundaries, swimming out toward the center as fairies stared out in concern. A few fairies, mostly younger, fluttered out over the water, whispering to each other as they watched the newts. For the most part, the newts paid them no mind.

It was difficult to find a flat enough place to land. Taking long enough that surely her smell was in the air, Dime was not surprised when Juni bounced up onto the edge of the platform barely before they'd landed. "Hey!" Dime warned. "You'll tip it over!"

Tum's chair was already empty beside her and Juni's white features sped by like a passing vision as Dime stepped down onto the moist soil. "Stern Eyes, hi." The older newt was hiding behind a tree, mostly. Dime went over to greet her friend, worried at how unsettled she appeared. Stern Eyes grunted and sort of threw her body against Dime's, wriggling in toward her. Dime sat down with her a while, just watching the leaves rustle in the trees.

They'd been through a lot in a short time. Juni had already run off with Tum, both squealing excitedly like the world were new. Being older, Stern Eyes had been impacted more gravely. Dime understood that. They sat there, together.

Maybe a take later, Juni and Tum returned. Juni set Tum in her chair, across from Dime and Stern Eyes, where Tum moved quickly into an intense conversation with Stern Eyes as Juni bounced around.

"Tell her we're working on expanding their land," Dime said. "We're working to explain to pyrsi why it's important, even if we can't get them to see that it's right. Eventually, they'll have to take stronger measures, but they are giving pyrsi a chance, first. I'm sorry that it's taking so long."

"I told Juni all that already, Ma-ma. She was showing me all the work she's been doing. I guess you gave them a bag?"

Dime rubbed her forehead. Ella's bag, yes, they'd given it to Stern Eyes. That first time, when she'd left.

"She used the bag to take her treasures—I think that's the best word—from her old burrow and she's been taking her time arranging them in the new one. I thought she just stuck them in the dirt, but she's making it sound like there's a whole ceremony involved."

"Does she want to show us now, or when it's done?" Dime asked.

"When it's done." As if caught, she added, "She said I was the only one allowed to see it."

Another newt ambled up, a huge being wearing a vine of dried leaves, draped like a scarf. Following, several others moved in and sat down.

"Oh, my," Dime said. She scooted herself straighter.

"I think they think this is a gathering. Since Stern Eyes is here and we came over. They think you called a thing."

Stern Eyes looked over at Dime, her expression tired.

Dime thought. *Music.* If nothing else, she always had faith in the sound. "Ask if they'd like a song."

"I already know that answer," Tum said, her voice still bubbling with excitement. "They love music. I sing to Juni all the time and it's her favorite."

Stern Eyes just blew a puff of air, then bent to rub her toes.

"Alright. Tell everyone to keep gathering, then." This was

pointless direction; it was a rather large group, now. A couple of young fairies hovered in the distance. Juni asked if they could join, and so Dime beckoned them over. "Do you mind sitting in the branches?" she asked them. "So the newts have room on the ground." The two fairies settled in on a long branch, their arms around each other's waists, looking nervous in the midst of so many newts.

"It's ok. They're very gentle. Though, I'd probably stay up there." She was worried about the fairies being scared, not hurt. The newts just weren't in the same place with consent.

Seeing some of the newts getting antsy, she looked at Tum, who was ready to translate. "My father is a storyteller," Dime said. "And I think if he were here, this is what he'd choose. Except—and Tum, make sure they understand this part—this is a song that requires participation. Now, is everyone ready? And don't try and translate the song. We'll let them enjoy it by the sounds." She glanced at the fairies in the branch. "We hope you'll join us."

After a round of clicks and whirrs and a couple of questions from the back, Tum nodded. "Go ahead, Ma-ma."

Dime cleared her throat. Oh, if her father could see her now.

> Monarch of the Clouds
> They call xem 'xe' for short
> Each day xe drifts around
> Each night xe drifts about
>
> Would you like to play a game, they say
> You'd have to drift on down
> Monarch of the Clouds, says oh
> You surely see my crown
>
> Perhaps you have an itch, xe says
> To be someone like me
> Who sails above the world each turn
> As lofty as can be

> No, no, our friend, we do not see
> A need to claim the air
> How could we play this game right now
> If some of us were there
>
> But don't you like to have nice things
> The Monarch touched xyr crown
> The nicest things are here, they said
> With friends, to share the ground

"Now this is where you can join in," she said. "When I say, 'yes, yes,' you echo that rhythm by clapping twice." The fairies poked each other giggling, looking less nervous than before, and Tum showed the newts what it meant, to smack their paws together. With the thick skin of their hands, it turned out the newts' claps were rather muted. But added together, they made a rather pleasant sound, like a deep drum.

Less like a drum, the newts had no sense of rhythm, and so each time she sang the line, there was more like a low thunder. It didn't matter. Everyone was having fun, and so she signaled her own hands to the fairies in the trees, so they saw when to do it.

> Yes, yes, (clap-clap)
> Yes, yes, (clap-clap)
> Our treasure is our friends
>
> Yes, yes, (clap-clap)
> Yes, yes, (clap-clap)
> Our friendship never ends

As it turned out, the newts grew entirely too excited by the whole exercise, and they kept demanding repeated iterations. Juni kept bumping Dime as she swayed, and Stern Eyes had joined a small group who were clapping along together. Dime was at the point she was never going to sing this song again by the time she finally managed to wind it down. Probably every newt who had moved thus far was gathered in a huge and now rather intimidating clump. The two fairies up above her had scooted closer to each other. She smiled at them reassuringly.

Some of the newts started to whine.

"What if we do one more song?" she asked Tum. "I'll try to make it one without an endlessly looping refrain this time."

Tum grunted something loudly, and the others repeated it out, like a stone rippling on water.

"They accept this deal." Her tone was sarcastically solemn, and Dime grinned at her.

"Hey, I do need to get back and plan those lessons. Ok, which song? I'll let you pick."

"Neighborhood," Tum answered without any hesitation.

Ah. Ma'Rorg's closing song. Also, a group song, though perhaps not suited for newt vocals. Ma'Rorg used to have the whole audience singing along, still humming the tune as they walked back to their towers or hopped into waiting toothcars. Honestly, Dime was still singing it.

She looked at her child, who had a bit of pleading in her eyes, hoping Dime would honor her request for *this* song. Dime knew that the terrible events at the Crossing—for all the good that came out of it had no bearing on the lives lost or the pyrsi who had witnessed it—weighed heavily on Tum. She was seeing a counselor who could help her talk through them, but, well, a little music could help too.

"Is everyone ready?"

Some newts jumped, knocking over other newts, and Dime was worried she'd have a full-scale thumb-plank display on her hands. Time, then, to sing.

> I love being me

The newts couldn't understand the words, but they were already perking up. Many were still clapping, as if the last song hadn't ended. She went on.

> I love that you're you
> I love that we can start a new bell
> Decide what we will do

One of the newts, understanding that Dime was bending her voice to make music, began to sort of howl, trying to match Dime's tone. This caught on quickly, as one, then another newt joined in. Soon the entire gathering of newts howled in different tones, with some still clapping, completely drowning out Dime's song. Squips began to chatter on the branches above and a flock of birds landed and began to sing and the insects made a chorus like the finest of string instruments, and Dime was starting to think every creature in the Heartland had joined them for Ma'Rorg's closing song. She imagined their song reaching Pito, and then Lodon. What if everyone in Ada-ji took a moment, and all sang together.

She wished everyone would join in.

Knowing that singing the words was almost moot at this point, as the howl of the newts overtook her own low voice, she continued to sing the song anyway. Tum knew the words, and was watching her mouth, being sure to sing along with her. Smiling at each other, they continued.

> If you'd like to talk, then talk to me
> If I'd like to talk, I'll talk to you
> If nothing else, we'll sing this song
> We'll sing together, happily—because—

They paused, for where the row of chimes would be played.

> I love being me
> And I love that . . .

It was important to almost whisper the last two words. It didn't really work with a chorus of howling newts, but to herself, and to Tum, she did it anyway.

> you're you

She rose from her seated position, trying to make it clear that her visiting time was up. Dime had considered that traveling here would not give her a greatly adequate number of bells to plan the next set of lessons. Now, glowing with the impact music could have, she was surely going to do it. Tikinal would help; he was the best when Dime got distracted. She moved over to grasp the handles of Tum's chair, and not trying to make a big deal that she availed herself of a small amount of valence, helped push her back over the branches and bumps toward the waiting platform.

Dime felt pretty sure she was licked a few times on her way out, with Juni barking indignantly, as they made it back and she positioned Tum into place. Then she accepted Juni's huge hug.

"I'll see you soon," she said, as Tum murmured beside her. She glanced out at a group of clapping newts. "Tell Stern Eyes we'll be back when we can."

She watched the young fairies fly back to their homes on the other side of the lake, perhaps to waiting parents, she could imagine.

Dime wondered what they would tell them.

"How were lessons?" Anathatu asked. "Youth, right?"

Dime pulled up her chair around the round table, along with Dayn, Tikinal, and Anathatu. Tum was visiting one of her new schoolmates in the village, but Agni had stayed behind, always seeming to enjoy the chance to peer out of the tower windows.

"They went well," she answered. "And, yes, this one was all youth. It was funny, when they first got together, everyone was looking to see who had wings, and who had tattoos, and comparing names and talking about hair and towers and clothes. Then once we started the music, those differences were still there, but they were now notes in the same song. Sounds right?" she asked her co-teacher.

"I've never been so happy." Tikinal didn't look up, but continued to assemble the game on the table. It wasn't quite as fancy a version of Treetops as the one he'd gifted her from the Seats' lounge, but Tikinal and his spouse both treated the old, worn set with reverence. Its small wooden board and game pieces had an almost yellow hue, contrasting against Ella's dark table.

Ella had offered to leave most of the furnishings in place for Dime and Dayn's use, as they'd been built specifically to the unique size and shape of the tower. Only the fourth-floor library furnishings had been almost entirely taken with her, as well as Ella's own drawings. Remodeling the cozy upper floor with its tall, slanted ceiling to be a music practice space for Dime was somewhere on her list. She'd offered Dayn half of the top story for whatever he wanted, but he'd said he had plenty of room in Tum's workshop, and she could use having a place of her own. Her mind always wandered thinking about how the room could be arranged, and after contemplating a few designs for raised cushions, she realized Tikinal was talking.

"And so the entire classification of strings will have to be reexamined," he continued. "Woods and reeds are a more extraordinary case. The solies have such little exposure to them. They do have flutes—made of metal!—but primarily they rely on what they call 'brass instruments'. More like machines than instruments if you ask me, but I've been intrigued by the euphonious melodies they conjure with them. Drums at least, appear to be universal. Everyone has some familiarity with the percussive classes. Oh!" He glanced at Anathatu. "I've been thinking about something. You know imbas? The keyboards that are struck with mallets." Anathatu barely concealed a tilt to his mouth, as if he'd lived with a music enthusiast for cycles but didn't know basic instruments. "The solies have something very similar but theirs are made with metal and produce an entirely different timbre.

"I've been thinking of composing a piece using both versions, and with influences of both styles. I mentioned this to the class, and they started improvising it on the spot. So now, I'm thinking, that will be one of our main projects—perhaps we can be granted rations, paynotes, whatever, to take the show to both cities." Tikinal turned to Anathatu with an excited smile.

Dime imagined the group of Aochs lined up with their varieties of imbas: large, small, metal, and wood, beaming their joy across Ada-ji. She looked at Dayn, knowing her face conveyed much of the same excitement Tikinal had just shown in gazing at his own spouse. "Thanks for letting me do this." She hoped he knew how much she meant it. The words weren't enough.

Dayn smiled and returned to sorting out the wooden squips.

"So are we learning the full rules this time?" she asked.

"I will attempt it," Anathatu said. "I'm not used to teaching the full game to ad'pyrsi."

"Oh, stop it," Dayn scolded. "I'm not going to be lectured on my lack of training with Treetops when you had no idea how a lamp worked."

The chimes that Dime had installed sounded, marking the bells, and Tikinal rolled his eyes.

"It's crude," Anathatu muttered as the chimes subsided, returning to the concept of a soly lamp. "And smoky."

"No, you know what's smoky," Dayn said, "is using wood pipes for warmed water!"

Dime knew that Dayn had considered it a great victory when he'd convinced the two fairies to allow the construction team to put a metal piping system into their tree home here. The tipping point had been when Dime pointed out that the closest repair pyrsi had no experience with wooden pipes, and calling in someone from over the cliff might not be the most timely solution with a plumbing emergency.

Unlike Dayn and Ador, who might keep a discussion going for bells, Dayn's arguments with Anathatu never lasted long. The writer was quickly distracted. Or perhaps used to diffusing arguments, as Tikinal was particular about details.

Besides, that reminded her, they had reasons to want to learn the full version. Ador and Batu had promised to visit in a turn or two when Tum was here, and they'd all play the game together. Dime wondered if she should let Luja know. Ve'd enjoy that. Yes, she definitely would. Perhaps Gorg could join ver. With that many pyrsi, they'd need to move to the classrooms. But what fun it would be.

"That owl you have is one of the finest pieces of carving I've ever seen," Anathatu noted.

Dime turned to look at the large owl, perched on a custom shelf Uchitar had made just for it. The shelf was cut from a dark, heavily grained burl from here in the old woods, contrasting the subtle flow of the owl carved from a colorful piece of Heartland scrap.

"My friend carved it," she said. Of everyone, Rock's future was the least decided. She'd turned down one opportunity after another, for now living off the stipend Sala had issued her, for what Sala called her heroism at the Meeting.

Once she'd thought about it, she realized that Rock was probably working with Ador, waiting for a chance to participate in the reorganized government. Rock played the long game when she needed to. Dime knew, whatever she did, she'd be great.

Their friendship had only grown stronger these turns, and Rock stopped by the tower fairly often. Always right when Dime needed her to. Last visit, Rock had talked her out of a funk by offering that they should go to the city to get matching hackberry tattoos. Dime touched the skin on her forehead, still dry but healing well.

She was so grateful.

Dime scanned the room, the homey, circular space, surrounded by old, narrow windows, and she couldn't imagine wanting to be anywhere else than here with friends, conversation, and a good game. A pot of brew cooled on the flatstone. A bird chirped joyfully on the ledge where Friend used to live, and Agni was curled into a ball under it, murmuring gently in her sleep.

By the door hung a tiny metal chain that would sometimes sway when someone entered. Her diamond pendant dangled there, in front of a narrow rectangular window, and when the light hit its slightly rounded edges, a host of rainbows would dance around the room, over the table, and spread into one that she really liked above the countertop sink.

Dime never wore it anymore. She didn't need it.

Everywhere she went, Dime would cast rainbows, herself.

Diamondsong: La Fine

About the Author

E.D.E. Bell (she/e) loves fantasy fiction and enjoys blending classic and modern elements. A passionate vegan and earnest progressive, she feels strongly about issues related to equality and compassion. Her works often explore conceptions of identity and community, including themes of friendship, family, and connection. She lives in Ferndale, Michigan, where she writes stories and revels in garlic. You can follow her adventures at edebell.com.

www.ingramcontent.com/pod-product-compliance
Lightning Source LLC
Chambersburg PA
CBHW032037180726
48284CB00008B/2629